The Book of Life

Book 2 of The Secret of the Tirthas

Steve Griffin

Contents

For Mum

Chapter 1: Plat Eyes

In the deep water there is pain and loss and endless, dispiriting grey, and then there are flames and snakes in skulls. There is the draw and pull and greed for the fire of life, the hunger that spans across time, the hunger for that which those who are living have now but do not comprehend and will lose, a hunger borne by those long gone, who sit in the swirling silts at the bottom of the water, soaked through to the core with cold and lifeless wet.

Theirs is a constant, fidgety greed.

*

They – whatever *they* were – were coming for her now, through the darkening swamp.

As she ran, bounding from one clump of bog grass to the next, weaving in and out of blackened tree stumps, desperately trying to avoid bubbling pools of greenish mud, Lizzie heard their mournful groans, interspersed with guttural snarls. *What were they?*

And *why oh why* had she been mad enough to go through another tirtha?

'You idiot!' she muttered to herself as she leapt into a mass of exposed tree root and had to scrabble about with her hands and feet to keep propelling herself forward. The stink from the marsh in front of her face was disgusting, all egg and wet and earth and toilets.

She realised she was losing any hope of finding her way back to the tirtha again – and had to force that idea straight out of her head. *One thing at a time.*

Glancing over her shoulder she saw the dark outline of one of *them* taking shape amidst the misty trees. From a distance he looked like a stumbling drunk, but after she'd transported from Miss Day's garden and come out of that reeking pool she'd seen him close up, and the eyes had assured her this was no ordinary man.

A groan came from her left and she turned to catch sight of another, smaller figure, wading towards her through a tract of smoking swamp.

Screaming, she leapt free from the tree roots and splashed wildly across a section of clear but thankfully shallow water. Through the dense latticework of branches she glimpsed another pale light like one she'd spotted earlier, but as soon as she began to hope it might be a house or car it vanished again.

'Help!' she shouted. Her heart bludgeoned itself against her ribcage.

Another of the creatures bellowed from a short distance behind her. She looked back in terror, catching a glimpse of the sickle twilight moon high above the trees and then seeing the haggard, slime-coated face of a man leering at her through the fog. And then, as she looked back to check where she was running she screamed again because there, standing right in front of her, was a young girl.

Lizzie skidded and slipped, and ended up on one knee in the water, staring up in disbelief at the figure.

The girl had a mass of very blonde, almost-white hair, and was wearing an old-fashioned dress embroidered with pearly beads. Her pale skin and rosebud lips were fuzzy, as if she were standing behind a muslin curtain. In fact her whole body was insubstantial, shimmering with soft light in the darkness. Her eyes alone seemed fully present, sharp and intense, dark brown verging on black.

That way.

The girl's mouth had moved, but Lizzie was sure no sound had come from it. *But she'd heard the words in her head.*

She looked in the direction of the girl's pointing finger into a gloomy mass of waterlogged forest.

'Wha...' she began, but the girl was gone.

Lizzie felt a cold hand on her shoulder.

She yelped and tugged herself down and away from the man behind her. He hadn't got a proper hold and she came free and once more she was running – running, running, *running* for her life, in the direction she'd been told to go. *By a ghost girl.*

In her panic, time seemed to disappear. At one stage she was dimly aware of losing her footing and going completely underneath the foul-smelling water, but she was so possessed that before she knew it she was out and fleeing again.

The next thing she knew another faint wisp of light was floating amidst the tight mesh of forest. She lunged onwards, thrusting branches aside, snagging her ankle, scratching the side of her face on a twig – and the light's intensity grew.

She let out a cry of joy when the mist cleared for a moment and she realised it was a house. With renewed energy, Lizzie thrust herself through a swathe of tangled bush and creepers and came out on to clearer ground.

The house was now only a few hundred metres in front of her. It was big – very big – with a long wooden porch and a steep tiled roof, each gable end finished with an ornate iron spike. But best of all, the thing that steadied Lizzie's panic-stricken mind, was the pale yellow light coming from the downstairs windows. *Someone was in.*

'Help!' she screamed, splashing through ankle-deep water.

Then, just as she came through a final patch of scrub and could make out the louvre shutters in the windows, there was a moan and another creature sprang up from a dark pool, its arms stretching out towards her.

For a moment, Lizzie froze. The figure in front of her was an Afro-Caribbean teenage boy, his chest broad and muscular, wearing only a pair of ragged shorts. At first he appeared completely normal, but then she noticed the milky film covering his eyes – eyes that remained fixed on her in a rigid, soulless gaze as he stumbled forward, arms and fingers outstretched.

Shrieking and diving sideways, Lizzie avoided the boy's awkward lunge. She charged for the house, as he roared and lumbered after her.

And now she was on solid ground, an un-mown lawn in fact, and with a brief sense of the surreal she noticed an old-fashioned children's slide and a paddling pool, half-full of rainwater and leaves. She looked up at the covered porch of the house and saw an empty hammock strung between the rafters.

'This way! Over here!'

A door had opened and, framed in the light, Lizzie could see the figure of a woman. She was beckoning in an exaggerated fashion towards her.

'Come on! Get in the house. Quick!' The woman's voice was low and urgent.

Behind her Lizzie could hear the boy, moaning and stumbling across the grass. Without looking back, she sprang up the wooden steps and charged along the porch to the woman, who stepped quickly aside and ushered her in. As soon as Lizzie was in the house, the woman slammed the door and drew several bolts across in rapid succession. Gasping for breath, Lizzie noticed a small animal skull nailed above the doorframe.

They were in a wide, carpeted hallway, hung with pictures and decorated with rich wooden furnishings. Several doors led off the hall, and right opposite them a broad staircase with polished banisters ascended to a landing.

'What you doin' out on the bayou on a night like this?' asked the woman angrily, drawing the last bolt at the bottom of the door. She stood upright, and looked down at Lizzie's face. She was a tall black woman with greying hair tied up at the back.

For once Lizzie was speechless. She'd been through so much in the last hour, all she felt was an enormous welling up of emotion. Worst of all, she realised, was the fact *she couldn't get back home*. She had no idea where the tirtha was, underwater, out there in the depths of the swamp, surrounded by those awful things.

Would she ever see her mum again?

Lizzie emitted a great, single wail, and began sobbing uncontrollably.

The woman stepped forward and wrapped her arms around her. She stroked Lizzie's hair and hugged her into her warm body.

'There, there,' she said, soothingly. 'Those plat-eyes won't be comin' in here, not tonight. Not with all I've done to keep 'em out...'

For a while Lizzie abandoned herself to the tears, feeling them flood hot and wet down her cheeks and soak into the coarse cotton of the woman's dress. She cried so long and hard it became difficult to breathe. *Everything was so awful, so terrible and unbelievable.* But after a while the combination of the woman's steady caress and soothing voice restored a little of her security. She stopped crying, and drew back. The woman held her by the shoulders and looked her in the eye.

'What's your name, girl?' she asked.

'Lizzie.'

'Lizzie what?'

'Lizzie Jones.'

'Well, pleased to meet you, Lizzie Jones. My name is Lola. I can't even imagine what you were up to out there on the swamp, but you got to promise me: you're not goin' out again tonight. You're stayin' here, safe inside with us.'

'Us?' said Lizzie, looking around the empty hallway.

'Yes, us. Take off those filthy shoes, and I'll bring you in to meet the young Miss. Grief! You don't look so good and you don't smell so good either. Never mind, we can soon get you out those clothes and cleaned up. But first – the shoes.'

Once Lizzie had removed her shoes and socks, Lola took her hand and led her down the corridor, which smelt of homely, polished wood, up to an elegant, panelled door. Lola turned the brass handle and waved Lizzie through.

She came into a large sitting room with a big, unlit fireplace. White louvre shutters on the windows sealed out the night. The room was lit by candles and lamps and decorated in a luxurious, old-fashioned style, with lacquered tables, a cream chaise-long, and a gilt-edged mirror above the mantelpiece. Framed black-and-white family photos flanked an ornate carriage clock on the mantelpiece, and Lizzie noticed a retro-looking brown phone on a nearby sideboard.

Sitting in front of the fire, in a wheelchair with her back towards them, was someone who Lizzie could see had a mass of curly, golden hair.

Lola cleared her throat, as a means of drawing attention.

'There's a visitor for you, Miss,' she said.

There was no response.

'Miss? Miss Caroline?' The figure remained motionless. 'Oh, she must have fallen asleep again...'

But just as Lola began to walk forwards, Lizzie saw the girl's hands reach down and grip the wheels. Slowly, the chair pivoted around towards them.

The girl was wearing a beautiful white cotton dress, embroidered with sequins and lace, and in her left arm she clutched a raggedy old wooden doll with feathers in its hair. A book was lying open on her lap. As soon as Lizzie saw the girl's face she gasped, recognising the pale, delicate features and dark eyes of the girl in the swamp. *The ghost girl!*

She barely registered Lola's next words:

'Lizzie Jones – meet Miss Day.'

Chapter 2: The Heart of Kashi

A Few Days Earlier: Kashi, The City of Light – India

As soon as he spotted the slight figure hurrying along the Marble Palace balcony Pandu knew it was *her* – the evil priestess, Lamya.

It was the fourth day of filming *The Heart of Kashi*, the sequel to the blockbusting *Rose of Kashi*, and he had been sitting patiently atop his elephant Ramses IV waiting for the actors Dick Pike and Vona Makkouk to finish a scene when Ramses had begun a deep and resonant rumbling. Pandu was immediately reminded of the only other time he'd heard his faithful elephant make such a noise – when he had stood confronting the fearsome cat-like demons attacking Lizzie beneath the palace walls.

The boy snapped out of his heat-induced daydream and scanned the crowded film set in the palace courtyard – but it was only when Ramses flicked his trunk up high that he saw the priestess with her cropped brown hair disappearing into one of the rooms that overlooked the courtyard. Despite the terrible heat he shuddered as if the air had turned cold.

Surely it couldn't be her? *She'd been in prison for months now, awaiting trial.* Whilst Pandu's friend, Inspector Raj Faruwallah, had realised Lamya's collaboration with the Pisaca could never be made public – *who would believe in demons and portals across the world?* – he'd built a strong case for her as the mastermind behind the priest Bakir's torture and murder.

A few people – a cameraman and a couple of sound technicians, as well as the stocky Dick Pike himself – looked round as Ramses continued to rumble.

'Is he OK?' asked one of the technicians, with an uncertain glance at the huge elephant.

'Sure,' Pandu said. 'Just keen to get back for his tea.'

'You're free to go as soon as this scene's over,' said the man, and turned back to his boom pole.

Pandu rubbed his hands nervously across the rough brown-grey skin of the elephant's back. 'Is it her, old friend? Only one way to be sure...' he muttered, swinging his legs up and lowering himself down the elephant's flank.

'Sanjay!' he called to the boy who was slurping lassi through a straw on the elephant next to him. 'Off to the loo – keep an eye on Ramses for me.'

'Sure,' said the boy, before resuming his slurping.

'Be good,' Pandu whispered into Ramses' ear, knowing full well that the elephant would – and then he darted off towards the main building of the palace.

With the largely uncontrolled chaos of the filming, Pandu found it easy enough to slip through into one of the shaded inner courtyards. He hurried past a marble

14

fountain feeding a pond full of yellow water lilies, then spotted a small wooden door that had been left ajar. Quickly, he slipped inside, taking care not to move the door in case the hinges creaked.

He found himself in a narrow, unfurnished corridor with several closed doors on either side. He scuttled down to the end and peered around the corner.

Excellent! A few more doors and then a flight of stairs heading up. *And only a small staircase, so less chance of it being heavily used.*

But just as he began his dash towards the stairs he heard the handle of one of the doors ahead rattling. With no other options coming to mind, he dived sideways into a deep-set doorway. He risked a quick peek down the hall and saw a servant coming towards him with a tray of iced drinks. The servant had just snagged the sole of his sandal and was looking down to right it – so he didn't spot the temple boy.

What should he do? If he opened the door he would be heard – and the man was coming straight towards him, so would surely see him standing there like a lemon in the doorframe...

The slip-slap of the man's shoes drew closer. Pandu felt sweat pricking on his forehead. With no time to think he kicked the door to make a noise as if he'd closed it, then stepped forward into the corridor just as the turbaned servant was upon him.

'Hey – cast and crew are not supposed to use those toilets!' shouted the man angrily.

'Sorry,' said Pandu, breathing a sigh of relief. The servant was a swarthy man, with several warts on his nose and cheeks. *Hardly your usual servant in a high-caste palace*, Pandu thought fleetingly.

'Your facilities are the temporary ones out in the courtyard! Get out now, Sabi will order you a good beating if he catches you in here!'

'OK.' Pandu dutifully followed the scowling man back down the corridor. The servant stopped towards the end and beckoned forcefully towards the small door Pandu had come in through.

'Off you go!' he barked, opening the door he had stopped by. He waited for Pandu to walk to the end and leave before he turned and disappeared into the room.

After a few moments Pandu came back in and ran down the corridor to the stairs. He leapt up them three at a time, past the first and second floors and then he was out on the third, the penultimate floor, the one on which he'd spotted Lamya.

He took off the smart shoes he'd been given for the film and stuck one in each of his back pockets, then crept carefully down the long landing. The corridor was punctuated by ornate niches carved into the walls. Most of the niches contained pedestals that were oddly empty of the statues and vases he would have expected to see on them.

He came to an open doorway and peered inside.

He saw a large, airy sitting room with two big archways leading out on to a balcony. Fierce sunlight streamed into the room through the archways. The left one was partially shaded by a portable screen, which was decorated with a picture of Lord Krishna playing his pipes to a group of adoring buttermaids. Long red curtains were tied back on either side of the archways.

He headed to the balcony and saw that it formed part of the long walkway along which Lamya had been hurrying. He peeped over the edge of the balcony wall and saw the swarming mass of the film set – the white-shirted cameramen sat on their elaborate cameras, the elephants and their riders all to one side, and the jostling mass of the crew in a circle around Vona, who was singing a wistful song.

Impressive as ever, he thought briefly, then crouched down and began to make his way along the walkway to the next room. Through an archway similar to the one he'd come through he caught a glimpse of book-lined walls – *a library* – before the sound of voices inside made him stop and hold his breath.

'... grateful to you for helping us,' said a refined, male Indian voice in English.

'It was my pleasure,' replied a similarly cultured voice with an English accent. 'Although I have to say it was a steep payment, even by British standards.'

'Yes, we're highly indebted to you,' said a woman's voice with a soft lilt, which Pandu immediately recognised as Lamya. 'But what I want to know is what you've been doing all these months whilst I've been locked in a cramped cell? Have you secured any Artefacts?'

There was a certain frostiness in the Englishman's response. 'I've been doing plenty,' he said. 'Much of The Book of Life is now translated, we know more about what's required, and...'

'What about the Mistress?' hissed the woman.

A pause, which Pandu imagined to be one of indignation. 'I have been through to Hundora and spoken with Papadris. He has lived with her for... oh, just about forever. He says there is a phylactery in the castle...'

'Phylactery? What's that?' said Lamya.

'If you wait a minute, I'll tell you,' said the Englishman. He took a deep breath. 'A phylactery is a vessel – in this case a portrait – which preserves the soul. We need blood from an Arch Witch – or at least a *witchkin* – magicked within an Artefact, to make it work. Papadris believes he can do it.'

'Whose blood will we use?' said Lamya.

'There's always your girl in England,' interjected the Indian man, whose voice Pandu suddenly recognised from his occasional tours of the film set – *Sabi, the owner of the Palace!*

'Yes, or the one trapped in Cypress House by...' began Lamya.

Hands grabbed Pandu's shoulders and pulled him back. Before he could even gasp an arm had locked itself around his neck and was cutting off his breath.

'Who are you?' hissed a man's voice in his ear. 'What are you doing?'

Pandu gagged and gulped, trying to speak.

The man began to force him forward towards the archway. Pandu pulled desperately at the arm locked around his neck but to no avail. The situation was helpless, and he realised he was going to be pushed into full view of the room's occupants.

And then there was a dull thud and the man's arm fell away from his neck. Pandu spun round to see the portly figure of Inspector Raj Faruwallah standing above him, with his assailant lying prostrate on the balcony floor.

His friend put his finger up to his mouth and mimed a *shhh*.

Wide eyed and still in shock, Pandu nodded. He glanced down at the man who had grabbed him and saw that he was young, with dark-rimmed glasses and a large mole on his cheek.

'Come on,' whispered Raj. 'I don't think they heard anything.'

Pandu nodded again, wondering why the young Inspector was wearing plain clothes as he followed him back down the balcony.

'Don't talk till we're back on the set,' Raj whispered as they hurried through the sitting room and down the stairs.

Soon they emerged through the half-open door back into the milling crowd of the film set, which was now closing down for the day.

'Hurry up and get Ramses,' said Raj. 'That chap might come round any moment.'

Pandu went and retrieved Ramses from Sanjay, and soon he was walking the elephant out of the palace gates with the Inspector at his side.

'How come you were there?' said Pandu, as soon as they were out of earshot of the guards.

'We've been following Lamya ever since she got out on bail,' said Raj. 'She's come here a couple of times. I had a quiet word with the film director yesterday evening, and he told the guards I was to be let in as part of the crew.

'No one knew why – or more importantly, *how* – Sabi managed to bail that witch,' he continued. 'As far as we knew there was no connection between them, they didn't even know each other. And as far as we knew, he didn't have two rupees to rub together – let alone the couple of crore needed to bail her. But perhaps this explains it – there's someone else involved.'

'Yes, and from the sound of it, that someone is English,' said Pandu. Then he added: 'You could have told me you were there!'

'I didn't want you involved again. *Don't* want you involved again.'

'You're not going to sideline me on this one,' said Pandu. 'If she's out we... we need to protect Albi,' said Pandu. The horror of all that had happened to his little brother with the demonic Pisaca flashed in his mind.

'Yes,' said Raj. 'Don't worry, I've already thought about that. I'm going to arrange for him to stay at my home with my housekeeper – at least until I find out what's going on.'

'And we need to let Lizzie – and Ashlyn – know,' said Pandu, thinking furiously. 'They might be in danger...'

'OK, we will,' said Raj. 'But let's not start a panic. Let's be sure we know what Lamya is up to first.'

'I'll help!' said Pandu.

'No,' said Raj. 'It's too dangerous.'

Chapter 3: The Ghost Girl

Lizzie stared in disbelief at the girl.

'But... you... I just saw...'

The pinch of a frown appeared between the girl's near-invisible blonde eyebrows. Lizzie was transfixed, staring at this vision before her, trying to be sure that she was just... *real*. That the fuzziness around the edge of her golden hair was just the fineness of the hair itself, softened by candlelight, and that her translucent white skin was just that – skin.

'You just saw *what*?' It took Lizzie a moment to process what the girl had said. And she recognised the accent which was, which was... *American*. She was American.

'I... I saw *you*... out there!'

The girl looked up at the black woman. 'Who is she?' she said, her mouth curling at the edge.

'I don't know, Miss – I was just checking the shutters in the hallway and saw her runnin' towards us out the trees, plat eyes hot on her tail.'

'She was lucky not to be dead man's meat, running round out there in the night,' said the girl.

'Hey – I am here!' said Lizzie. 'You don't have to ignore me.'

The girl looked appraisingly at her. 'Where've you come from?' she asked. Before Lizzie had the chance to reply she added: 'You stink!'

'I... I...' Lizzie felt the hopelessness of even trying to explain. Tears began to wet her eyes again.

'Look, why don't I just go and get her cleaned up first of all, Miss,' said Lola. 'Then when the poor girl has got herself together, we can talk to her properly.'

'Whatever,' said the girl, abruptly swinging her chair back to face the fire.

Lizzie felt the tears streaming down her cheeks as she was led away by Lola.

*

The woman took her up the plush staircase to a green carpeted landing with large doors on either side.

'First we gonna get you out those clothes and into a nice hot bath,' she said. She stopped for a moment and put her hand up to her mouth. 'Let me see now...Green, Cream or Red – no *this* one,' she said, and steered Lizzie into one of the nearby bedrooms.

When Lola turned on the light and Lizzie saw the bedroom through her tear-warped vision she thought she was in something out of a film. The room was as big as hers and her mum's bedrooms put together, with a beautiful four poster bed and a dressing table with an antique mirror, webbed with spidery dots and dark smudges. The wallpaper was printed with hundreds of finely drawn birds, ranging from tiny wrens and thrushes, to blackbirds and glorious herons, to peacocks and plump partridges. A pair of intricate white china storks stood on a small table beside the bed.

'The Bird Room,' announced Lola. Smiling, she added: 'Just in case you hadn't guessed. Used to be Mr Charles'...'

Whilst the room was undoubtedly wonderful it did nothing to distract Lizzie from her overwhelming sense of misery. Tears poured from her eyes and she emitted strained, wincing sobs.

'Come on, come on,' said Lola, hugging her again. 'You get out those filthy clothes, leave 'em in a pile over there by the door. There's a dressing gown on the back of the door, it'll swamp you but it'll do. I'll go run you a bath.'

With that she held Lizzie by both of her arms for a few moments and looked her in the eyes, then turned and headed out. Lizzie heard the floorboards creaking as Lola made her way down the landing. Moments later there was a clattering followed by a rushing sound as a plug was stopped and taps were turned on.

Quickly peeling off her gunk-soaked clothes, Lizzie wrapped herself in the giant silk robe and sat down on the bed. She was wracked by a few more sobs, then she wiped her eyes with her wrists and told herself *enough.* She had to get a grip.

Still alive is still in the game, as her dad used to say. Right now, she wasn't convinced. *What would her mum think when she woke up in the morning and Lizzie wasn't there?*

And what about Mr Tubs? Already she was missing them with what felt like a physical pain.

She looked around at the room, thinking how she'd never been anywhere as nice as this in her whole life. The pillow cases and bedspread had more elegant looking white birds stalking amidst bamboo shoots, on a cream background. The bed posters were made of a rich, dark wood, engraved with thorny roses, fruit and more birds. On the bedside table were two photos, both in black and white. One was of a thin-faced, pale man, his light hair greased back from his forehead. He was very handsome, in a vintage kind of way, and a cigarette hung out of the side of his mouth. The other was also of a man, a younger man, with finer features and more lush, wavy hair swept back from his face. He wore an old-fashioned looking pair of horn-rimmed glasses.

A sudden clattering of the louvre shutters in the windows made her jump.

Just the wind, she thought, and then thought of those terrible creatures roaming about out there in the night. She shuddered, and hurried down the landing to the bathroom.

'This bath's just about ready for you now,' said Lola. 'We might have trouble with the electrics, but water's one thing we do have plenty of round here.'

As if to mark her words, the room and landing suddenly darkened, throbbed with light, and went pitch black again, before returning once more to light.

'Huh!' said Lola. 'There you see – don't know my own powers!'

But for all the woman's bravado, Lizzie thought she caught a glimpse of uncertainty in her eyes for a moment. Then Lola said:

'Come on – in you go!'

Lizzie wondered if she meant for her to have the bath with her still in the room. After a moment she realised that clearly she did.

'What's a matter, Miss? You modest or somethin'?'

Lizzie nodded.

'I've been round long enough to see *everythin'*,' said Lola. 'And you're never gonna get all that muck off unless you get some help. Come on.'

Embarrassed, Lizzie climbed out of her gown and submitted herself to all kinds of scrubbing, soaping and shampooing. The luxurious hot bath was exactly what she needed to help her – at least for a few minutes at a time – forget about the chase and the fact that she didn't know how to get home. Lola seemed to sense this and stayed silent. Lizzie was filled with gratitude. She knew that soon enough Lola and the girl would be asking her all kinds of impossible questions, but Lola's peaceful quietness was just what she needed right now.

But as she stood up in the bath and Lola started to dry her down with a big white towel, her own questions began to spring up in her mind.

'Who – *what* – were those things?' she asked finally.

'Out there? They were plat eyes. Men a long time dead who did bad things and got brought back out the swamp by Hoodoo magic.'

'Hoodoo?' said Lizzie. 'Do you mean Voodoo?' She was thinking of a James Bond film she'd seen, full of skulls, snakes, heat and black magic.

'Hoodoo's what we know round here. Hoodoo and Voodoo ain't the same thing at all, they're different kinds of belief and magic.'

'How many of those *plat eyes* are there?'

'Who knows. More'n enough to make us stay put.'

'What do they do to you?'

'You don't want to be givin' yourself nightmares, child.'

'Why don't they come in the house?'

'That'll be me.'

Lizzie looked at her. 'What?'

'I'm no stranger to the ways of Hoodoo myself.'

Lizzie considered this for a moment, then said:

'Can't you call for help?'

'The lines are all down. We had some bad winds last... last night, I think it was. Because of the Big One that's coming. Mr Miles, when he gets back, he'll sort it all out.'

'What about your mobiles?'

Lola gave her a funny look. 'Mobiles? What's mobiles got to do with anything?'

Didn't they call them something else in America — if that's where she was?

'Cell phones? Can't you get any signal?'

27

'This ain't no prison, child. On the other hand, with all those plat eyes you can take that back!' Lola chuckled at her own joke.

Feeling flummoxed, Lizzie decided to let it lie. Lola had finished drying her and the heat from the air and the bath were suddenly making her feel sleepy – *immensely* sleepy. She yawned.

'Are you hungry?' asked Lola

'No – ate before I... came out,' she said.

'Now listen, you mustn't go takin' offence to anything Miss Caroline says to you, because ever since her eleventh birthday she's not been at all well...' Lola began. She stopped for a moment and stared at Lizzie, then added: 'I think you might need a little sleep before anythin' else.'

'Might be... a good idea,' said Lizzie, and the last thing she remembered was emitting another enormous yawn.

Chapter 4: Breakfast with Miss Day

When Lizzie woke between crisp white sheets, the window shutters were glowing with early morning light.

She felt as if she'd been clubbed repeatedly round the head during the night and it took her a while to sort out her strange, fitful dreams and momentary memories of sharp and terrifying wakefulness from the morning's steady, solid reality. Her mind echoed with mournful bellows, rushing wind, clattering and cracking sounds, with dreams of awful men who grinned and laughed at her, and with deep, strong scents of... of... *the musty furnishings and books of home.*

When the full memory of the previous evening finally came back she emitted a long groan and lifted her arms up across her eyes.

Not again...

How was she going to get back home? She checked her watch on the bedside table: 11.10, it said, no doubt stopped for good by its one-hundred-percent drenching in *a stinking bog.*

Her mum would surely be awake by now and panicking. *What would she think when she went into Lizzie's room and found the bed un-slept in?* And when she went down stairs and found Mr Tubs in his usual place under the stairs, meaning Lizzie wasn't out with him?

Knowing her mum, she would go crazy with worry. She'd be straight on the phone to her fancyman, Godwin Lennox, and she might even call the police. Godwin would search the gardens with Chen Yang, the young Chinese guy he'd employed on her mum's behalf as their gardener. Briefly, Lizzie fumed at the memory of Chen's regular intrusions into *her* garden. It was all because of *him* that she was in this predicament. *Yet another decision her mum hadn't consulted her on.*

Before she even had a chance to find the tirtha in the swamp and get back home there'd be some massive manhunt going on throughout Hoad's Wood and the Herefordshire countryside. With a sense of grim irony Lizzie remembered the manhunt – *or rather boy-hunt* – last November for Albi, which she'd first heard about from the farmer's boy, Thomas Bennett. But then the thought of Albi back safe in India with his brother Pandu and Inspector Faruwallah temporarily eased her worry. After all, she had – *with a little help from her friends* – defeated the she-demon Pisaca, the treacherous Lady Eva Blane. *And if she'd done that, surely she was capable of sorting out her current predicament?*

She took a deep breath. Why couldn't this tirtha have been like the Easter Island one, where there was no one around and all she'd found was that nice little statue she'd taken home as a souvenir and put on the desk in The Tower?

She sat up in the bed. She had to get going, there was no time to lose. It was morning now, she had to get out and try to find the tirtha again. It would be much easier in the day, she would surely remember the stagnant pond she'd been transported into. She would recognise the lie of the eerie trees and grassy hummocks around it. And as for those *plat eyes* – well, they weren't exactly the fastest kids on the block. If she kept her wits about her she was sure she could outrun them. And who knew, maybe if they really were created by some *Hoodoo* magic perhaps they couldn't come out in daylight? Yes, if she was quick enough she might just get home before her mum sounded the alarm.

As she leapt out of bed she realised she was wearing a cotton nightdress that Lola must have put her in before putting her into bed. *What a nice lady*, she thought momentarily. *Shame I won't get the chance to know her better.*

She rushed over to one of the windows and flung open the louvre shutters. Beneath her a potholed drive led away from the front door into the woods. The raggedy overgrown lawn with the children's playthings was bathed in the soft light that comes just before sunrise. Beyond the lawn Lizzie noticed a low wooden fence with several broken sections – one of which she must have come running through the night before – and then the start of the rough wet grasses and moss-hung trees of the swamp.

Was she really going back out into *that?*

Of course she was! She had to get going fast, to keep one step ahead of her doubts and fears. Looking round the room she saw that Lola had laid her out a fresh change of clothing on a chair. Lizzie hurried over and checked it out. A pale blue dress, underwear and long white socks, and a pair of brown sandals. Not the kind of stuff she'd ever choose to wear, not that it mattered now.

Must be that awful girl's, she thought as she yanked them on and strapped her feet into the sandals. Luckily, even though *Miss Caroline* was younger than her, Lizzie's smallness for her age meant everything fitted well enough.

Once she was dressed she couldn't help but take a quick glance at herself in the full length mirror that hung beside the door.

'Alice in bloody Wonderland...' she muttered as she went over to the door and carefully twisted the brass handle. She eased it open, relieved when it didn't creak. She leaned into the corridor and looked left and right.

No one around. She scampered down the landing, thankful for the plush patterned carpet, then trod slowly down the stairs. She noticed portraits on the wall, of fat Churchillian men and elegant, high society ladies. One included a whole, finely dressed family in front of the house, with a black man in a red uniform, standing off to one side like a servant. Once, Lizzie might have been impressed by such affluence but now, after Eva, she had no more truck with the lavish displays of the rich.

32

At the bottom she crossed the hall to the front door and stopped for a moment, taking in the skull that had been nailed up above the door. It looked like a rat's, or maybe a snake's skull, and it was daubed in something dark red. Lizzie wrinkled her nose, hoping it was paint but guessing it was blood. *Did Lola really think she could do magic?* That said, something must be keeping the plat eyes out.

She moved over to the door and began to draw back the first of the bolts, fraction by fraction. Just as she had completed the first and begun on the second, she heard a bang from down the hall.

Someone was up!

She heard footsteps coming through the nearby room towards the door. Quickly she pulled the second bolt and was reaching for the third when the door swung open and Lola was standing there, a duster and spray bottle in her hands.

'Wha'...' said the woman.

Lizzie pulled the final bolt and put her hand to the door handle but then was barged sideways by the woman and crashed into a small table. On the floor, Lizzie quickly twisted round and propped herself up on her hands. She stared up defiantly at Lola.

'Who are you?' shouted the woman, her expression a febrile mix of anger and confusion.

'What?' said Lizzie.

Immediately, recognition dawned on Lola's face. 'Oh – it's you,' she said.

'Of course it's me!'

For a moment Lola seemed puzzled then the anger returned to her voice as she said: 'What do you think you're doing?'

'I'm going out,' said Lizzie.

'No you're not!'

'Yes I am!'

'If you open that door the spell goes down and I'll have to spend the whole morning fixin' it! What if there's a plat eye standing right outside waitin' for you? You want to be a corpse's breakfast?'

'I need to get out!'

'Over my dead body! You're not jeopardisin' the safety of this house – of those who've so kindly taken you in an' protected you from the evil outside.'

'But I need to get home...' said Lizzie quietly.

An awkward silence was broken by a thin shriek from the end of the hallway. Lizzie and Lola looked around.

'Miss Caroline...' muttered Lola. Fear showed in her eyes as she looked back at Lizzie.

Realising that Lola was scared – no, *terrified* – for either the girl's safety *or* of Lizzie opening the door, Lizzie said: 'Don't worry, I won't.'

Lola nodded silently then hurried off down the hall, calling out: 'I'm coming, Miss Caroline...'

'At least, I won't *now*,' Lizzie added under her breath.

Lola reached the door at the far end of the hall and disappeared through it. Lizzie heard her starting to tell the girl not to worry, but then she shut the door behind her and the hall went quiet.

Feeling a sudden sense of pity for Lola, Lizzie began drawing the bolts back in place. *What must it be like, looking after a spoilt little brat like that?* Then she remembered what Lola had told her when she got out of the bath, about Miss Caroline being ill. She wondered what kind of illness she had. Something bad enough to put her in a wheelchair. She resolved to be more considerate, and to bite her tongue if the girl was rude to her again.

But what was with the apparition out on the swamp?

As she felt a familiar constriction in her chest – *panic* – she hurried away from the front door and headed back into the dark living room at the other end of the hall. Her mind was overloading again and she needed to distract herself. She went to one of the windows and swung open the shutters. The sun had risen and was picking out silver dewdrops in the long grass. The small yellow slide was patched with green and brown lichen, and clearly hadn't been used for years. She scanned the mossy branches of the trees beyond the fence, but couldn't see a single plat eye lurking in the gloom.

Time for all good zombies to go bye-byes, she thought, with a small, semi-hysterical chuckle.

She checked the latch on the window. How easily would it open? *She might have to find out later.*

Now the room was lit, she went over to the phone and picked it up. It had an old fashioned dialling disc on the base that Lizzie knew how to use – but as soon as she put the handset to her ear she could tell there was no line. She tapped the small black buttons that the receiver rested on but there was still no dial tone. Lola had clearly been telling the truth, not that Lizzie had any reason to doubt her.

She went over to the TV and studied it for a moment. The screen was small, but it was huge at the back, big as a boulder. Lizzie looked around for the remote. Unable to find one, she looked at the set itself and saw some buttons on it. After pushing and turning a couple there was a sudden electrical hum, a grey line sliced the middle of the screen, and then a black and white picture of a horse talking to a man kicked in.

'You don't want to do that, Wilbur...' said the horse.

Lizzie found the switch that changed the channels. There was an advert about a woman cleaning her pans with a new type of sponge, a film of cowboys herding cattle, and then a fierce-looking man reading the weather forecast with no map.

'Winds are buffeting coastal regions, and Carla is expected to hit later this evening...'

Black and white. It was all in black and white. *What happened to the colour?*

'Making yourself at home?'

Lizzie spun round to see the blonde girl had wheeled herself in through the open doorway.

Remember, she's ill, thought Lizzie. 'Sorry,' she said, switching off the TV.

'We need to be careful about opening the shutters,' said the girl, wheeling over and peering out of the window. 'They could break in.' She pushed one of the louvre shutters to, but didn't seem bothered enough to

36

close it properly. She pointed to the other window in the room and said: 'Lola has protected those ones. You can open them.'

As soon as Caroline pointed the windows out, Lizzie noticed the familiar tiny skull bulbs nailed above them. Obediently, she went and opened the shutters to those. For the first time, she looked out on to the other side of the house, seeing a large yard with several ramshackle wooden outhouses and a big green tree in the centre. There was an old-fashioned blue car parked up against one of them, with at least two totally flat tyres that she could see.

'Do they come out in the day?' she asked.

The girl shrugged, then said: 'Lola's made us some breakfast. Come through to the dining room.'

She swung round, uninterested in any response from Lizzie. Amazed by the girl's lackadaisical style, Lizzie followed her through half-open double doors into a room with a large table and plush pink chairs patterned with roses. All the windows, including two French doors, were *under protection* in here, and the shutters were open.

Lizzie sat down at the table and surveyed the spread. There was a bowl with fruit – a couple of red apples, a thin slice of melon and a handful of figs – and a couple of pieces of toast with small dollops of butter and jam in dishes. Lizzie suddenly realised how starving she was and reached forward and grabbed a piece of toast – then remembered her manners and offered the toast rack to her host.

'No, thanks, you go ahead – I'll just have some melon,' said Caroline.

Within moments Lizzie's mouth was full with jam-laden bread. As she gulped the food down she became aware of the girl watching her.

'Sorry,' she mumbled.

'No, you must be hungry,' said the girl. Lizzie glanced at Caroline and for the first time her opinion of the girl softened slightly. It was the first thing she'd said that showed any awareness of other people having feelings too.

'Can I have the other piece?' she asked when she'd finished the first slice of toast.

'Sure – go ahead.'

Lizzie noticed Caroline had barely touched the painfully thin slice of melon on her plate. 'How long have you been stuck in here with those things outside?' she asked.

'Ages,' said Caroline. 'Feels like forever!'

'And it's just the two of you?'

Caroline nodded.

'Where's your mum and dad?'

The girl's back stiffened. 'Mama and Papa are dead.'

Lizzie stopped chewing. 'Oh no – I'm really sorry,' she said. She noticed the girl's doll again, as Caroline drew it more tightly into her lap. It was a very old, dirty looking thing, with googly eyes under its grey feathery headdress and – *yuck* – what appeared to be a carved snake dangling from its mouth. It looked homemade.

Caroline shook her head. 'Don't be. Mama died in childbirth and Papa died when I was eight. I hardly ever saw him, and anyway...'

'Anyway what?' Lizzie's mind buzzed with the little that she and her friend Ashlyn had discovered about the garden from her Great-Uncle Eric's journals before she accidentally discovered the trigger for the portal. About *Miss Day's* Garden... She would have to think it through later.

'He was a coward.'

'Oh.' *What a weird thing to say about your dad.*

The awkward silence that ensued was broken by Lola coming into the room with a silver pot.

'Coffee?' she said.

Lizzie looked up hopefully. 'Do you have any tea?'

Lola chuckled. 'You English! It's no joke, is it?'

Lizzie didn't know what to say.

'No, sorry, we don't have any tea. How about juice?'

Lizzie nodded. 'Thanks.'

Lola disappeared and came back with a small glass of orange juice, which Lizzie drank down quickly. She then picked up an apple and took a deep bite out.

'Lola says you're waiting for your brother to come home?' she said.

'Yes, Miles. He went to get emergency supplies from Baton Rouge last... a few days ago. He'll be back soon. He'll sort everything out.' Caroline looked out of the window, as if expecting his car to reappear there and then.

'Baton Rouge,' Lizzie repeated. 'That's, err – so, France...?'

'What?'

Lizzie blushed under Caroline's look of incredulity, noticing the hostility return.

'Sorry, erm, just thinking. Baton Rouge, yes, must be in the, err... region? Yes, the region of...err...' *No, that was as far as her French geography went.* She knew there were regions in France, but couldn't name a single one.

'You don't even know where you *are*?' said Caroline.

'Yes – yes I do!' Lizzie blurted. 'Just, not sure of the, erm, the, err, the *name* of the region...'

'You're crazy,' said Caroline, and rolled her eyes.

'I got lost,' said Lizzie. 'Lost from my folks. Now, I'll need to get back to them so I need to know.' She stared down at the white table cloth, realising any explanation was hopeless. *She had nothing to lose.* 'Where are we?' she asked, in a small voice.

Caroline looked at her appraisingly. 'You really don't know, do you?'

'No.'

There was a moment's icy silence, then Caroline said: 'It's an old plantation called Cypress House. Eighty miles south of Baton Rouge.' Lizzie continued to stare.

'In the Mississippi bayou. Louisiana. The South.'

Lizzie looked at her, her brain catching up slowly.

'The United States of America? Have you heard of them?'

Lizzie felt her cheeks burning with shame, and for a moment she felt like she would cry again. *America, like she'd first thought.* It was the *Rouge* bit that had confused her.

But Caroline didn't seem to want to stop: 'The Good Ole U.S. of A.? Yankee doodle dandy and all that? The old colony?'

'OK, I get it!'

They stared at each other for a moment until once again Lola came back in.

'You finished?' asked the woman.

'I'm going to do some reading,' Caroline announced. 'Take me to the library, Lola.'

'Yes Miss.'

Lizzie scowled at the girl's precociousness. *If she was Lola she'd swipe her.*

'What am I going to do?' asked Lizzie as Lola dutifully wheeled the younger girl out.

'Amuse yourself,' said Caroline. '*Indoors.*'

Lizzie twisted towards the window so the girl wouldn't see her torrent of mouthed insults.

And then they were gone and she was alone in the dining room, looking out of the French doors at the dusty yard with its giant oak tree. *What was she going to do?*

She realised she was going to have to try and get out but... not just yet. She was sure that even though Lola had gone, she would be listening out for her trying to make another break for it. And, whilst she was sceptical that Lola's magic wards had any real power, she'd seen enough in her escapades in India to know that weird things – *really* weird things – did happen in the world. So she couldn't risk being responsible for breaking a magic protection and letting those repulsive creatures into the house. What would they do to Lola – and to Caroline, who wouldn't have a chance of getting away from them in her wheelchair? But as soon as she realised she couldn't break out easily the frustration of knowing her mum would be up and about and panicking *right now* made her hair prickle with heat. *What could she do?* she wondered again desperately.

Nothing fast. She was just going to have to sit tight and think some things through and – *and what?* Look round the house? *What then?*

She gazed out of the window at the broken-down car in the yard. It had a long roof and a long, narrow bonnet, with big wheel arches at the front. The wheels had dozens of thin metal spokes and small, rusted hubcaps. The car looked like something out of the black and white cop shows her gran used to watch on satellite. Everything here was just so... *old-fashioned.*

She wracked her brains for any clues she might have about this place. Her Wiccan friend, Ashlyn Wickes, had been diligently digesting Great-Uncle Eric's copious, illegible journals over the last few months. The witch had told Lizzie about how Eric's aunt, Evelyn, had had problems with her brother Charles. Evelyn had argued with Charles a lot and eventually taken a profound dislike to him for some reason. This come to a head when he'd used the tirthas – probably *this* tirtha – to escape from something. That was all Lizzie could remember about him.

And then there was the garden – *Miss Day's* garden – itself. Whilst most of the gardens had been well maintained, this one hadn't. Her great-uncle had clearly not been bothered with it. She had first taken an interest in it when she'd heard Chen Yang wrestling with the snagged-up gate one day. His grunts of frustration as he tugged at bindweed and brambles had attracted her attention from the Edwardian Path where she'd been playing ball with Mr Tubs. When after a few minutes she crept round to see what he was up to she had to be quick to hide behind one of the large menhirs because he was already coming back out. Once he disappeared down one of the hedged corridors she went into the garden and found that he'd cleared a small path through the horrendous tangle of weeds and brambles. Struggling through the vegetation, she came to the centrepiece of the hedged *room* – a beautiful, slender tree with pale white-green leaves. At the base of the tree was a damp, dirty straw doll which she guessed from her previous experiences of the garden rooms might act as the trigger mechanism for this portal. Which of course it had, as she'd found out to her great misfortune, when she came out with a torch after her mum had gone to bed that night. *Only to be transported – once she'd figured out that she had to hold the tree and doll at the same time – right into the depths of a stinking quagmire.*

She wondered what Chen had been up to in the garden. She retained a deep suspicion of Godwin and his *lackey* due to their relationship with Eva, the awful Pisaca herself. It was possible that Chen was just doing his job gardening, but she wasn't so sure.

Lizzie wondered whether Caroline was *the* Miss Day that Evelyn had named the garden after, but after a moment's reflection realised she couldn't be – Evelyn had died years ago, so it must have been Caroline's... mother, or even grandmother? Making her Charles' daughter or granddaughter.

And those few things were the sum total of all Lizzie knew about this tirtha. So all in all – *not very much*. She sighed and slumped her face and arms dramatically forward on to the freshly laundered table cloth.

Once again her life had turned into a freak show overnight – and she only had herself to blame.

Chapter 5: The Bureau

Lizzie spent the whole morning looking round the house but she still couldn't find one thing that she would truly call *modern*.

What was it with this place? It was like it was caught in a time warp or something. Although there were plenty of signs of wear – the sofa's protective sleeves were fraying and there were deep ruts in the carpets where the wheelchair had been – everything appeared beautifully made and of the highest quality. But there were none of the modern electrical things that she would expect to see in such a wealthy household. There were no tablets or computers, no wifi box or mobiles, no flat screen TVs or any sign of satellite. There were two old-style phones, the one she'd found in the sitting room and another in the hall – and just the one ancient television, which when she'd flicked it back on had been showing the same creepy talking-horse show.

What was going on?

She checked the carriage clock on the mantelpiece and realised it was after one o'clock, but still she didn't feel hungry. The heat had built tremendously throughout the morning and unsurprisingly there was no air conditioning in the house. She was tired but oddly restless, the whole place felt as if it was charged with some kind of peculiar atmosphere. She was wondering where Caroline was when Lola appeared in the sitting room and offered her some lunch.

She sat on her own in the dining room and had a small bowl of fish soup and half a roll with butter, but she ate more from habit than appetite. She guessed she must still be full from breakfast. Halfway through her meal, Lola came in and sat down with a bowl of soup.

'I don't seem to have got off to a good start with Caroline,' said Lizzie.

Lola slurped a spoonful of the steaming brown soup. 'As I said, never you mind. She's not well.'

'What's wrong with her?'

'Disease of the blood,' said Lola, staring into her soup.

'Of the blood? You mean, like haemophilia or something?'

'Yes ma'am, that's it.'

'Oh – poor girl,' said Lizzie. She felt awkward for a moment, both out of guilt for having been angry with Caroline, and from Lola having just called her *ma'am*. She'd never been called anything like that in her life. And, despite being a servant, it was the first time Lola had used such a formal expression with her before. Something wasn't right.

Something? More like everything! said a little voice in her head.

46

'Why haven't you got colour TV?' asked Lizzie.

'You think we're made of money?'

'They don't cost that much. I didn't even know you could get black and white TVs anymore.'

'Huh.'

Lizzie sensed she was starting to get on the wrong side of Lola too, and the panic and desperation lurking just below the surface began to rise again. She needed to feel the woman's support and had to make sure she didn't sound critical.

'The weather man said something about a storm coming. Do you know anything about it?'

'Storm! Not a storm, girl. That's Carla, the hurricane. She ain't no storm. She is the Big One.'

'A hurricane? What are we going to do?' Lizzie saw her hopes of escape retreating away even further.

'Nothing. Just batten down the hatches as always and pray to the Lord. And *for* Mr Miles.'

'When's it going to hit us?'

'Should be gettin' the advance winds tonight.'

'Oh my God.'

Lola looked her in the eye. 'Yes, indeed, child. Yes indeed.'

*

After her meagre lunch, Lizzie felt a headache developing with the oppressive heat. As she headed up to her room to rest she worried about what she was going to tell her mum when she finally got back. Perhaps she could tell her that she'd run away from home for a few days, maybe to Wales or Hereford, but then decided to come back. Having her mum think she was becoming a problem child would be better than telling her the truth. The wretchedness of her situation and having to lie vanished briefly when she thought she could also hint that Godwin had been part of the reason for her running away. And then she felt bad again, for having such deceitful and manipulative thoughts.

God, if she'd known life was going to get this complicated as a teenager, she wouldn't have spent so many years wishing she could hurry up and be one.

Back in the room with all the birds she sat down on her bed and wiped her forehead with her powder blue sleeve. She was literally dripping! She didn't think she'd ever felt this hot in her life, not even in India. She was just about to collapse on to her back when she noticed a small door in the corner of the room near the window. Thinking that she might have her own bathroom where she could at least splash her face with cold water, she went over and opened it.

Beyond was a small room that was empty except for a chest-high wooden cabinet of shiny, black-red wood, with a padded chair in front of it. Disappointed that it wasn't an ensuite, Lizzie shut the door and turned around. She wondered whether she could even be bothered to traipse down the landing to the bathroom. *It was so hot, and her head was killing her.*

And then a thought flitted across her mind. *It wasn't a cabinet, it was one of those dainty antique desks that you pulled open.*

Despite her headache, her curiosity got the better of her and she went back into the little room. She walked up to the fancy desk and tried to prise it open. The fold-down section wouldn't budge, and she noticed that it had a tiny keyhole.

What was so special it needed locking up? she wondered. She looked around to see if there was an obvious place to keep the key.

She opened the two drawers at the bottom of the desk but they were just full of old papers and notebooks. Then she glanced around on the floor, but there was nothing there. Finally she latched her fingertips on to the desk rim again and tried pulling harder, just in case she could force it open.

No luck. She went back into the bedroom and looked around on the dressing table and side tables, as well as in all the drawers she could find. No keys. She kicked off her sandals and lay down on the bed, sighing.

Just one more thing to add to the long, long list of minor – and not-so-minor – mysteries and frustrations she'd experienced ever since she'd inherited her great-uncle's cottage.

*

When she woke up some time later from a deep slumber she felt anything but refreshed. Her mouth was parched, her hair was matted to her head with sweat and, whilst her headache had subsided a little, she still felt... *woozy*. God, that was one of her mum's words, she used it when she'd had too much to drink. Lizzie never thought she'd think it, but she missed her so much. *How was she ever going to get out of this place?*

With renewed dread, she realised that it was starting to get dark. She sat up on the edge of the bed and shook her damp hair. Then she stood up and walked over to the window.

The moon had appeared again, slicing a yellow sickle out of the dark blue sky. The trees beyond the smashed fence hunkered down with their trailing moss like primordial, semi-aware beasts. Like monsters, she thought, trolls or ents, something that pretended to be simple but could suddenly turn quick and bad. Lizzie shuddered, realising she didn't need to use her imagination – there were real monsters lurking out there in the shadows.

She had to get out. She needed to be in her own bed. *Tonight.*

She hurried downstairs, determined to make Lola let her out of the front door. Lola could then do all the bolts and reinstate her spells or whatever she had to do whilst Lizzie used the last remnants of daylight to retrace her steps and find the tirtha again. She could do it – she *would* do it – and she'd outwit those stupid plat eyes and follow the route she would somehow innately remember and find the pond and take the plunge and then she'd be home again, all within the hour...

She thought of Mr Tubs, his sweet little ginger-brown whiskers and moist dark eyes and his ticklish licks of joy. *And of her mum, holding her tight in one of her crushing hugs, the ones Lizzie had studiously avoided ever since her dad died...*

But as she approached the half-open sitting room door it was Caroline's voice that she heard and her frenzied sense of determination evaporated.

'You'll keep me safe, won't you Sally Ally, my beautiful baby, sweetheart...' the girl was saying in her soft Southern accent.

Who was she talking to? *Lola?*

Lizzie peered round the edge of the door and saw that the wheelchair was in the same place as the previous evening, in front of the marble mantelpiece. Caroline had her back to her and was looking down into her lap, her halo of white-gold hair reminding Lizzie of the ghostly apparition out on the marsh. For a moment, she wondered if she might be going crazy, or if this might just all be a bad dream.

'Little charm, you help Lola keep the plat eyes out – oh, and let us know, please, let us know what we should do with *her...*'

'You mean me?' said Lizzie, ignoring the creepy crawly feeling on her skin.

Caroline's head twisted and she thrust her chair round to face Lizzie.

'Spying on us now, are you, you little witch?' she said, her dark eyes glaring.

'Us?'

They both looked down at the raggedy old doll in Caroline's lap.

After a moment's bewildered silence, Lizzie said: 'I have so *got* to get out of this place,' and turned and marched into the dining room, where Lola was setting down two plates of fish with greens.

'I need you to open the front door and let me out,' she said.

The woman stared at her for a moment and then said: 'No.'

'I'm going, whether you like it or not!'

Lola shook her head slowly. 'You'd be dead before the food was cold.'

'I don't care – I want to go home!'

'Sit down, have somethin' to eat.'

'No!'

'Sit down, Miss. You need some food inside you.'

As Lizzie stared into the gentle brown eyes watching her back so steadily she realised that everything was going – her resolve, her composure, the dryness of her eyes... And once again she found herself in Lola's strong and reassuring arms as she bawled her eyes out.

A sudden banging made her stop crying, and both she and Lola were looking round at the closed shutters on the French doors.

'Only the wind,' said Lola, because they both knew they'd feared it was the plat eyes.

The shock helped distract Lizzie and, with a sense of partially regained pride, she sat down at the table and looked down at her food.

'You've got to understand, this is very, very strange for me,' she said in a strained voice without looking up at Lola. She dug a hefty silver fork into her greens, but realised that she still had no appetite.

'It's very strange for all of us,' said Lola, and turned and walked out of the room.

Lizzie wiped her nose on the back of her hand and stared at the grey skin of the fish. *No appetite at all.* Perhaps she was ill. She had to eat something.

She picked up a small lump of fish and put it in her mouth. It tasted nice, but she could only manage a few mouthfuls before she gave up and let the fork clatter on the plate. She stared morosely at the shutters, hearing the wind shaking the trees outside. So, the storm was coming. That was going to make it even harder to escape. She felt as if she was standing in front of an unassailable wall – and then the next instant it was as if she was on a precipice about to fall off. Her head seemed to swing on the inside.

She was feeling dizzy.

A thin, metallic squeal made her turn her head as Caroline wheeled herself into the room and took up her place at the table opposite her. Lizzie watched as the blonde girl began to pick inconsequentially at her food.

'No one eat anything at all round here?' said Lizzie.

'It's too hot,' said Caroline. 'I can never eat in high summer.'

'Hmm,' said Lizzie. She really was feeling strange – hot, and her head was starting to spin. It was a bit like the emotional turbulence of passing through a tirtha. *May as well go for it,* she thought. 'So, how did you do it?'

Caroline looked at her uneasily. 'Do what?'

'The ghost-girl thing. The fuzzy edges. You know. That spook-on-the-swamp look?'

'What are you talking about?'

'And the garden. You're a Miss Day, too, aren't you? Is it named after your grandma or mum? What's all that about, then?' Even as she spoke, Lizzie realised she shouldn't be talking about the garden. *She felt weird.*

'Are you crazy?' said Caroline.

'You know damned well I'm not crazy. What's it all about? Tell me! What's in that locked desk in the room off mine? And why do you talk to your doll? Is it Voodoo or Hoodoo or whatever–*doo* you like to call it? In short – *what the hell is going on in this Freaksville?*'

'Don't you raise your voice at me!'

'I haven't even started yet! And the phones – what's with the lack of mobiles – or any other modern stuff? Is this place caught in a time warp or something? What's going...'

'Lola!' screamed Caroline. If possible, it seemed as if she'd become even whiter than she was before. 'Lola!'

Lizzie heard the floorboards creaking as Lola came down the hall towards them. Then she noticed something strange happening to the young girl in front of her. She was starting to shake a little, and her dark eyes were going funny – sort of out of focus, and then rolling upwards. Lizzie wondered if she was going to turn into the ghost again – but then realised that something was wrong – *definitely wrong.*

'Are you all right?' she said, beginning to stand up.

Next moment Caroline was convulsing, but before Lizzie could do anything Lola was in the room and

54

catching the girl as she slumped forwards out of her chair.

'What is it?' said Lizzie.

'Can't you see? Heavens! She's having a fit,' said Lola.

'Oh... what shall I do?'

But as Lizzie stood up her own dizziness returned in force and she had to grab the table to stop herself from falling over.

'I... I don't feel well either,' she managed to say, and then she collapsed.

Chapter 6: Mr Paterson

It's all noise, howling, grunting, rattling, crashing, an odd little dream-whimpering... and broken images, snarling little girls with white faces and black lips and tentacles for arms and legs, green-skinned men with frustration and malice and pale death in their eyes, then a moment of warmth and peace with the smell of a woman's sweat and of doggy fur and a shaking and jumping of legs at the gallows moment, the moment of lurching away from sleep... the smell of mud and rancid water, flashes of light in the darkness, a licked hairy leg and leathery paw pad, and then suddenly, in slow motion –

a sensation of rising up, up from the hot damp bed into the room, the shutters glowing soft grey with moonlight, and then turning slowly as she levitated to look back on... *herself*, a figure crouched in foetal position, now stilled and with an easing of the brow, an image of a girl in deep, calm sleep, it's *me* –

and then a leaping of the heart and a vicious snarl and sweat and sleep and loss – white flashing through the room, a booming sound, the raging wind, more groaning and grunting and a shout outside – and then sweat, burning and sweating, and sleep and loss again...

*

She was moaning. Hot and moaning.

Light had returned to the room. She was in bed, caught up amidst clammy sheets.

The light was daylight, soft strips of daylight, bright lines on the dark shutters. Not the white-blue light of the night, the lightning light of the storm. That was gone. The winds had dropped. It was quiet. *So much for the hurricane.*

She was thirsty. Her head hurt. She turned her face sideways.

There was a full glass of water on the table beside her. Weakly, she propped herself up on an elbow and reached for it. She began to drink. She had to take small sips, not the big gulps she wanted to take.

She was ill.

A fever. She had a fever. She'd had something like this before, the flu, the Christmas two years ago when she'd been bedbound for nearly three days. It had ruined her Christmas. *The last Christmas she had with her dad.*

She would have cried if she didn't feel so ill.

She fell asleep again.

*

When she woke again she felt disorientated – but nowhere near so feeble. She couldn't tell what time it was, but the room was brighter and warmer, despite the shutters still being shut.

The water had miraculously refilled itself – surely Lola's doing – and she drank it down more quickly this time. She wanted to get up, but her limbs still felt weak. She remembered Caroline's fit, and felt the shadow of remorse. *She had been too hard on her.* Something was definitely going on here. She didn't think the girl was lying, although she was sure she was hiding something.

The next moment she heard something she really hadn't been expecting – the sound of voices outside, and then the opening and slamming of a vehicle door!

Forgetting her weakness, she sprang from the bed and hurried to the window. She flicked up the catch and flung the shutters wide, just in time to see a large, pale yellow truck driving out of the yard. And behind the wheel was a man, a black man wearing blue overalls and a white cap.

Dust plumed up behind the van as it headed off down the pitted drive, away from the house.

'Lola!' shouted Lizzie. 'Lola – Caroline! There's a truck – it's going!'

She rushed to the door and flung it open. Lola was coming up the final couple of stairs on to the landing.

'Did you see? There was a man outside, in a truck. He was talking to someone...' said Lizzie, running up and grabbing the woman's arm.

'You need to get back in bed, Miss,' said Lola, pushing her back.

'But there was a man in the yard – in a truck!'

'Yes, yes, but come on now, back into bed with you,' said Lola, with a firm expression.

'Did you see him? We have to stop him! Oh, it's too late, he's gone, he's gone and we won't be able to...'

'That was just the grocer an' odd job man, Mr Paterson,' said Lola. 'Come on, now, you...'

'What?'

Lola stopped trying to push her backwards.

'What did you say?'

'He's just the grocer, brings us fresh food. Mr Miles hired him.'

'*Just* the grocer? Just. The. Grocer?' Lizzie stared at the woman, who seemed not to be able to look her properly in the eye. Then she shouted: 'You know him? Just tell me that you told him to get help. Please tell me that.'

Lola continued to look down sheepishly.

'You *didn't* tell him to get help? You didn't tell him to get help! Agh!'

'He's just the grocer, we need to wait for Mr Miles to get back.'

'What? What's the difference? We just need to get out of here! Why did you let him go?'

'Don't you be taking that tone with me,' said Lola.

'But...' Lizzie struggled to get the words out, she was so exasperated, 'but he – he could have taken us out of here, away from this hellhole, back to somewhere safe!'

Lola was silent.

'Didn't you think of that? Surely you must have thought of that!' Lizzie stared up at the woman and then looked away, growling with frustration.

'Or he could have phoned the police, called help, gone for someone. What were you thinking? Why did you let him go? We're surrounded by Swamp Things and you let our one chance of escape go. Nothing round here makes any sense!'

'Enough!'

Lizzie stepped back from the woman's furious look. Her own anger vanished with the shock of Lola's venom, and she suddenly felt an immense weakness in her legs and stomach. Before she could collapse, the woman had caught her and helped her back into her bedroom.

'I... I just don't understand,' she muttered, as Lola eased her down into bed.

'Don't think about it now, child,' said Lola. 'You've got a fever and you need more sleep.'

'But...'

'Just relax, I'll get you some more water.'

'But we need to get out...'

'Yes, child, we will. When Mr Miles comes back.'

As Lola left the room Lizzie stared blankly at the closed shutters, overcome with disbelief and bewilderment.

*

She woke again later with a start, staring at the dark canvas of the linen canopy above her bed.

She realised she must have slept again, a much more deep and calm sleep and, as she stretched her limbs she realised that the aches had gone and the fever seemed to have subsided. She still felt uncomfortably hot but after a moment's reflection realised that that was just... *normal*. It was like an oven here in Louisiana.

She sat up and downed the warm glass of water by the bed. Then she went over and opened the shutters. It was still daylight outside, but the sky had clouded over and a light breeze shook the mossy beards of all the creepy swamp trees. She could hear some shrieking and splashing within the wood and scrub, and after a few moments a large white bird with dark wings and a long neck flapped up above the canopy, its face and neck lizard-like, ugly and grey. Lizzie wondered whether the storm was coming back.

She had to get out of here.

Lola had put a fresh brown skirt and mauve blouse on the chair. They were dreadful, but at least they weren't quite as bad as the pale blue dress. She put them on quickly and went up to the door. Lola had obviously left it slightly open so she could hear Lizzie from downstairs if her fever got worse or if she shouted. Lizzie pushed it open and stepped out into the landing then stopped, as she heard voices in the hallway – or possibly the sitting room – below.

'...she's got it, I reckon. She's got the blood.' This was the low voice of Lola.

'How would you know?' said Caroline.

'It's the way she looks. She's sharp, but there's somethin' else. She sees through things, she's got vision.'

'Well, I don't know how you'd ever tell for sure, Lola. I think you're guessing, just because of what you know.'

'Hmm, I know. I know these things, child.'

'Maybe we should give her the Book? If it's *her*, it might help her to help us? There might be something in it that triggers something in her, or reminds her of something?'

A pause.

'No, I don't think we should do that. I think we should leave things as they are for a while. See what happens. In case it ain't *her*.'

'OK – but she knows there's something in the bureau.'

'No worries, she won't find it.'

'How do you know?'

'I've hidden it.'

Another pause.

'Lola – we are going to be all right, aren't we?' For once, Caroline's voice sounded more vulnerable, uncertain.

'Yes, of course, Miss. Everything's going to be all right, you take my word for it. Soon as Mr Miles is back.'

'He... he *is* going to come back soon, isn't he?'

'Yes, Miss.'

The silence that followed lasted, so Lizzie turned about and tiptoed back into her room.

She felt a lot better, her fever really had passed – if it even was a fever, and not just some terrible reaction of her whole system to the shock and anxiety of the last couple of days. She knew now, with every part of her being, that she needed to get out of here.

She went over to the window again. She looked out at the garden, at the yellow paddling pool full of leaves and gunk, and then at the porch. At the wooden slats of the porch... *below her.* Quickly she looked up and around the window frame. No nailed skulls, no totems of any sort... And then she realised: *Lola didn't protect the upstairs windows.*

There was obviously no need to – those lumbering doofuses didn't know how to climb!

It was only a metre or so drop to the porch roof after she'd opened the window and clambered up on to the ledge. She didn't even need to drop down and risk making a noise – she was able to let herself down easily on to it.

The porch roof was a sturdy construction, slightly sloped to let the rain run off but not at all difficult for her to creep along quietly, heading towards the opposite end of the house from the sitting room where Lola and Caroline were. When she reached the far end she got down on her hands and knees for greater stability and crawled down to the eave.

An iron gutter ran along the edge of the roof and drained into a down pipe fixed to the corner post of the porch. The gutter was sturdy but clearly old, and had rusted severely in places. Clumps of black-green moss clogged it up at several points.

Lizzie thought it would take her weight.

Glancing apprehensively at the swamp to reassure herself there were no plat eyes around, she peered over the edge of the roof to see how far it was down to the ground.

No problem, she told herself, ignoring the jelly feeling that had returned to her legs and was reminding her of her collapse the previous evening. *No problem at all.*

And with that, she grabbed hold of the gutter head and swung her legs out over the edge. Her feet slipped down the pipe and suddenly she was in a position in which she was off the roof and holding on to the pipe with her hands and feet, entirely reliant on the strength in her arms and legs.

'Whoa!' she said as she managed to stabilise herself.

Luckily the adrenalin had overcome her wobbliness and she felt strong enough to proceed down the pipe. She focused on taking one hand down at a time, her feet falling quickly into place each time she slid a little further down. As she descended she glanced along the length of the verandah, at the wicker chairs and tables and a hammock tied up towards the sitting room end. *No sign of the dynamic duo.*

Then, just as she was halfway down, there was a tortured, creaking sound and the pipe broke away from the wooden pillar. Lizzie fell backwards towards the ground, somehow managing to twist herself around at the final moment to land on her shoulder instead of flat on her back.

'Ow!'

It hadn't been a long fall, and it was more shock than pain that made her cry out. She climbed quickly to her feet, rubbing her shoulder and glancing at the drain pipe that now hung out in the air at a forty-five degree angle.

Had they heard? She realised she had no time to lose and ran past the slide and out towards the gap in the fence.

At the last moment, just before she disappeared into the swamp, she glanced back over her shoulder and saw Lola standing at the window in the hall, a look of panic on her face.

Chapter 7: Following The Priestess

Pandu's head fell to the side and jerked back upright almost simultaneously, as he fought back the mighty urge to fall asleep.

He had been sitting on a narrow flight of stairs since midnight, watching the derelict Temple of Kali – the scene of the terrible battle with the Daginis, and the death of the kind old priest Bakir, who had strived so hard to protect Pandu's brother Albi. *And the place where Lamya was still presiding priestess.*

He was worried about Albi. If Lamya was up to no good again he couldn't bear the thought of his brother being somehow dragged back into it. *Albi had suffered so much with the Pisaca.* Pandu was only partially reassured by Raj having taken his younger brother into his home. He also knew that he needed to visit Lizzie and tell her about Lamya – soon.

But despite his fretting, he was starting to doze off again when he suddenly heard the sound of footfall. He looked round just in time to see a lithe figure emerge from an alleyway and cross to the temple. It was her, the priestess, for sure! *He knew she would come back here eventually.*

He checked his phone: 3.37. At least three hours before dawn. He could try texting Raj – but knew that the Inspector would be angry with him for getting involved and spying. Raj would tell him to get to safety, which was the last thing he intended to do. After a moment's reflection, Pandu stood up, stretched his aching legs, and then, keeping in the deep shadows of the surrounding buildings, scurried over to the side of the cupolaed temple. As he approached, he noticed the outline of the hunched monkeys asleep on the rooftop, and prayed that they wouldn't hear him and wake up.

When he reached the temple he stopped, held his breath, and listened.

Nothing. Not a sound. *What was she up to?*

Whilst the temple had been closed officially for five months now, since the death of the priest, the police cordons of the crime scene had long since been taken down and Pandu knew that people were beginning to do their *puja*, their daily worship, there again. Was that what she was up to? Was she trying to get back down into that hellish cellar where so much atrocity had taken place? *And if so, why?*

His questions would remain unanswered for in the next moment she re-emerged and it was only the fact she headed straight for the steps that saved him from being seen. He didn't release his breath until she'd reached the top of the stairs.

And then, without a moment's hesitation, he set off in pursuit of the Kali priestess.

*

It wasn't long before Lamya reached the waterfront, just to the east of Man Mandir ghat.

Pandu was relieved she'd headed to the river, because he'd been having real trouble following her. There was barely any moonlight, so he'd been relying increasingly on the sound of her footfall, the skid and clip of her sandals on the street, to keep on her track. A couple of times he'd had to rely on guesswork as to which way she'd taken. But his intuition had been right – she was heading for the Ganges.

After she descended the steps to the main riverside promenade she turned right and began to head up river. The Ganges was nothing but a mass of blackness, interspersed with the odd whorl of grey – but its smell, strong and soil-like, maintained its domineering presence even in the night. As he followed her Pandu passed saddhus and dalits, piled up in small heaps for extra warmth or snuffling and snoozing alone. More people slept in their rowing boats, moored to the ghat and gently rocking in the river's current. Occasionally he passed someone still awake, staring out at the blue-black horizon above the river, or sitting by a small fire in front of a makeshift shrine.

Just like the old days, Pandu thought, as he followed Lamya on to Dashashwamedha ghat, the place where he'd done his first piece of lookout work last year, waiting for the Pisaca and then for Lizzie. At the time he'd not known anything about the magical tirtha in the old Brahma temple, which he now used to secretly visit his new friends Lizzie and Ashlyn in England.

And then his skin started to crawl, the closer and closer they got to that sacred place.

Surely she wasn't... no, she couldn't be...

Pandu stopped and watched with horror as Lamya, still a hundred metres or so ahead of him, reached the protruding temple and stopped. Quickly, he dropped into a crouch as she turned around to check no one else was about – and then she began inching around the narrow ledge that led to the entrance of the temple, which jutted out above the river.

She was! *She was going to use the portal.*

With a sense of alarm, Pandu reached into his pocket for his phone.

Now he was going to have to call Raj.

*

She was trying to find – *get this* – a pond. And not just any old pond, no. *A pond in a waterlogged swamp.*

As Lizzie tentatively jumped from one dry-looking tuft of grass to another slightly-less-dry-looking tuft of grass she continued her battle with the onslaught of withering thoughts in her head. Why had she left the (relative) safety of the house? Did she really think she could find the tirtha when it was *underwater*? Would the plat eyes get her and eat her alive? She sighed as she realised all her questions fitted neatly into one overriding one: *how did she ever manage to get herself into these situations in the first place?*

She looked all about at the still, stagnant waters, broken up only by patches of cotton grass and blackly-scarred, monolithic tree trunks that tapered as they rose toward frayed, feathery crowns. There was something about the stillness, the heat, the odd pillars of the trees that reminded Lizzie of a place of worship – a rundown church, or more likely one of those battered old temples she'd come across whilst exploring Kashi. It was all kind of... *eerie*.

Except of course, it wasn't truly still or silent. There was the occasional trill or shriek of a bird, the odd bluebottle bombing past, and every so often a particularly unpleasant cloud of midges would appear from nowhere and invade her eyes and ears. Once in a while there was a faint swish of water, which she found very unsettling and had to tell herself was just a fish. But mostly it was quiet. *Quiet and hot.*

The one good thing was she hadn't got soaked yet. *Oh yes, and there was one more good thing, how could she have overlooked that one:* ever since she'd dodged – with one solitary, piercing shriek – the flailing arms of the one near Cypress House: *No Plat Eyes.*

But she was keeping her eyes peeled. And not just for them. This was after all the Mississippi bayou, and she knew there were alligators and snakes in abundance here. She'd seen the films or watched the survival documentaries that her mum loved or just somehow or another taken it in as a kid. Was it anacondas or pythons that constricted you in America? And what about the poisonous ones? Despite the heat she felt her flesh crawl with goose pimples.

Keep the terror out. That was the only way to keep sane in a situation like this. Keep the terror out of your mind.

Out of your mind... How fitting.

Now then, orientation. She had travelled more or less in just two directions only since leaving the house. First she had headed in a straight line for the clump of trees where she was almost – ninety-nine percent, *easily good enough odds* – certain that she'd come across the young Miss Day in her spectral guise. From there, she had turned approximately forty-five degrees and headed in her second straight line for about ten minutes to... *here.*

So – was this where she'd come through the tirtha?

She spotted a small oval-shaped expanse of blue-black water surrounded by clumps of grass and black soil. Could that be it? Her heart beat quicker with excitement as she drew near to it. Yes, it seemed to fit the bill. She'd definitely come up on to a piece of dry ground just like this, she thought, pushing her feet into the wiry clumps of sedge.

So – what was she going to do? *Jump in?*

She felt a forest full of butterflies take flight in her stomach.

She couldn't think of anything worse than leaping into that stinking pool of water.

And then – because that was the kind of person she was, brought up by the marvellous, courageous father she'd had – she jumped in.

'Jeepers!'

With a small splash she was standing ankle-deep in what was effectively a large puddle.

Immediately she spotted another one, just a couple of metres away. *That must be it!* She strode over and this time tested the depth with a small stick that she pulled out from a nearby tree root. The pond was deep, much deeper than the one she'd just made a fool of herself in. Hoping that, if this was the tirtha, it would activate with a simple jump like the Kashi one, she leapt feet first into the pool.

This time she did go in over her head. As a confusion of silver and brown bubbles streaked over her eyes she felt her feet bang against the squelchy bottom and for a fearful moment her left foot seemed to stick in the mud and then it was free and she was propelling herself upwards and out again into the calm, sunny day.

She grabbed hold of the bank and caught her breath.

Try again.

Once again, she pinched her nose and plunged down and for what felt like ages jabbed at the bottom with her feet, taking care not to push them down too far, hoping that her world would suddenly break into subtle magic.

She came up again, gasping for air. Limp strings of vegetation crowned her head. She swiped them away and tried the bottom one more time.

Moments later she was out on dry land, prostrate on her back, staring up at the milk-blue sky, her chest heaving up and down as she regained her breath and composure. The silky mauve blouse clung unpleasantly to her skin, covered in flecks of green.

Finally she stood up and, wiping her hair back from her forehead, turned and looked around and spotted *here,* another distinct pool of water, and another *there,* and one more a short distance away *over there,* and that looked like one *there,* and *there* and *there...*

Slowly, she shook her head. *Was she going to have to jump into every last one of them?*

And how did she even know that this was the place? Initially she'd felt sure it must be, the lie of the landscape had seemed just right. But now she began to wonder. She didn't think there had been quite so many trees over there to the right, and she was certain she'd run *that* way through what surely must be a way-too-deep stretch of water.

Maybe she was just wishful thinking? She so *wanted* this to be the right place that she was attributing more correct features to it than was really the case. After all, she was at heart a city girl, who'd only lived in the countryside for less than six months and that was the *English* countryside. *What on earth would she know about making your way through an American swamp?*

With a renewed sense of heaviness, she sat down and realised the full hopelessness of her position.

And that's when she felt sharp nails dig into her scalp.

Chapter 8: Lost on the Bayou

The plat eye had got hold of Lizzie's head like a bowling ball and was using it to try and lift her off the ground. She had to scramble with her knees and feet to make sure he didn't break her neck.

'Get off!' she yelled, grabbing his wrists and trying to pull his hands away. His long yellow nails, caked with blood and mud, raked away at her scalp.

'Ahh!' was the only response.

'Get off me... you... freak!'

As she was pulled higher she managed to kick back with her heel into his knee. The creature stumbled, one of his hands came off her head but immediately grabbed her arm. She swung round and found herself staring into his godforsaken face.

He was a middle-aged white man wearing blue overalls. He had tanned skin and a wiry, salt-and-pepper beard. His brow was creased deeply down the middle – so deep, it was like a wound – and his blue eyes were sunk in their sockets. His expression flitted between harrowed, empty, and frenzied, just as his actions too seemed to change moment by moment. Now he was forcing her down, then holding her steady for a second but staring off into space, then shaking his head and once again pushing her down on to the ground.

'Get off me, Mister!' In her terror, Lizzie fleetingly imagined what a strange man might do to her. The fear made her redouble her efforts, and in his next distracted moment she managed to break her arm free and jab him on the nose.

'Uh!' he grunted, and she saw blood run down from his nostrils into his greasy moustache.

But his reaction was to shake her very hard and for a moment she was half senseless and her knees buckled underneath her. As she crumpled one of his arms curled around underneath hers and then she was crushed up against his side and he was dragging her away through the swamp.

'Stop...' she gasped, trying to get purchase on the ground with her feet, to push herself away from him.

'Ahhh...' he moaned, yanking her sideways and even closer into him.

'Who are you, what do you want? Get off me...'

The creature sniffed deeply, then coughed. Lizzie noticed a small knife in a holster on his belt, right beside her cheek that he was crushing into his waist.

She had never hurt anyone in her life.

Or at least not intentionally. She'd knocked the old priest Bakir down the steps of the ghat when he was about to strike Pandu with his staff – but she hadn't meant to hurt him. And that was it.

Could she stab a man?

A man who was deranged, and dragging her forcibly who knows where, perhaps with the intention of drowning her in an unseen pool in the midst of a swamp – or *worse*...

She whipped the knife out of its sheath and sliced at the hand that was gripping her like a vice.

Everything then seemed to happen in slow motion. She could see right next to her eye the way that the skin had opened up across the man's knuckles – but it took a few moments for the bright blood to emerge. The man slowed as he was wounded, but only reacted properly when the blood started to pour.

He cried out, and let her go. He raised the injured hand into the air and studied it with a look of confusion.

Lizzie looked briefly at the knife then threw it away. She sprang up from the mud and ran for her life into the nearby trees.

*

After running through the swamp for an unknown period of time she realised she was hot, filthy, damp, and lost. Most definitely lost. And she was starting to feel... *shaky*.

She had run for as long as she could into the waterlogged forest, away from the crazy woodsman or plat eye or zombie or whatever the hell you would call him. But as she'd run, she'd become increasingly certain that he wasn't following her. She remembered the look of shock and astonishment on his face as he beheld his injury. That had obviously been enough to snap him out of whatever crazy notion had got into him.

But here she was now, lost, *lost in the swamp*. It was still daylight but the sun was lower in the sky and the white mid-afternoon glare of the light had gone, to be replaced by a softer, more orangey-yellow sheen on the leaves and parched brown trunks of the trees. Be nice if I had a camera, she thought, then felt tears prick her eyes. *How could she be so pathetic as to joke to herself when things were this serious?*

If she wasn't careful, she could die. The list of hazards was never-ending. Snakes, alligators, starvation – *although as usual she didn't feel hungry* – plat eyes, quicksand, drowning, going out of *her tiny little mind...* she was going to have to use all her wits to survive. But as soon as she thought that she realised it was a lie she was telling herself. She was going to have to be *lucky* to survive. Very lucky. That was all. She couldn't think of anything constructive to do to help decide her fate. Besides keep on keeping on, that was.

As she waded through the oily waters, her heightened sense of watching for danger made her increasingly aware of the subtle wildlife of the bayou. She spotted small, green stripy turtles bathing themselves on stumps, and one swimming in the water that had a black stipple-ridged shell, which made her think at first that it was an armadillo. She saw ducks and geese and was stunned when she came out on to a broad expanse of water and saw dozens of beautiful, pure white birds with long necks and curved bills, all

78

standing in the water. She wondered if they were small storks.

At one stage her heart stopped in her mouth as she realised that a thin, olive-grey snake with a bright orange band down its back was swimming right across her path. Its mouth was wide open and there was a small speckled frog in it.

After a while the sun clouded over and a soft but steady breeze got up. She remembered the talk of the hurricane and wondered if it was still coming. Maybe this morning had just been the lull before the storm? *Yet another thing to add to her ever-growing list of worries.*

The one thing that was keeping her going was that she had no idea how big these swamps were and, thinking positively, she must surely come to a river or road – or maybe even a house – soon. This was, after all, America, a developed country with plenty of people living in it. Millions. *Hundreds* of millions. Surely she must come across some sign of civilization soon? Somewhere where there might even be such a thing as a telephone that worked, where she could phone home. Again she found herself chuckling to herself as she imagined a conversation with her mum.

Hi Mum, it's me.

Lizzie! I've been worried out of my mind – where are you?

Louisiana. Can you come and get me?

She stopped, sure that the water ahead had shimmered slightly.

Her heart leapt, filled with terror. Was it an alligator, or another snake? Or maybe there was a submerged plat eye, waiting to jump up at her.

But no, there seemed to be nothing there. Just a faint *fuzziness* on the surface of the water. And for that matter, on the fine spray of the pine needles on the branches above it. She was reminded of the odd lights she'd seen springing up and then disappearing in the distance on her first night. Cautiously, she edged forward.

The blurriness became less obvious as she drew closer to it, although if she focused her eyes long enough there was still clearly something there. She wondered if maybe it was her tiredness, but as she looked to the side and behind her everything seemed normal, the same as ever.

What was it?

Given that her situation was pretty damned desperate, she decided to move forward into it. What was the worst that could happen? *She kind of wished she hadn't asked herself that question.*

For a moment she was heading forwards and then she was heading sideways. She shook herself and tried moving forward again – but again was wading gently to her left. She tried harder, but the same thing happened again. *She could not walk forwards.*

What was going on? She hadn't felt anything strange at all – she'd simply found that she had been subtly, unobtrusively *redirected*. There was something, some line in the swamp, that she couldn't cross. *Weird.*

She wondered if this might be something to do with the tirtha. From everything she and Ashlyn had learned from her great-uncle's journals, they all seemed to exist in sites that had been held sacred throughout the centuries. If that was so, the one she'd come through here might well have been sacred to the ancients, but it had certainly been lost to modern humans a long time ago – perhaps when the area ceased to be dry land. But perhaps this one had some kind of larger dome of power that somehow led to this kind of... *force field* at the edge?

Yeah, and perhaps a big blue baby with wings was juggling turtles over there behind those trees.

What did she know? She might as well speculate on the mind of Newton, as her dad used to say. Or was it *like a dog on the mind of Newton?* Why did he used to say that?

After a moment's confusion, she decided she would follow the strange phenomenon. What had she got to lose? she asked herself a second time.

Besides her sanity, that was.

*

After maybe half an hour of following the strange field she still hadn't discovered anything out of the ordinary.

Just more bog, trees, and rank smelling water.

What's more, it was definitely starting to get darker. The pearly light of the clouds had gone and their greyness had started to seep into the trees, making everything much duller. She wondered how long it would be until it got properly dark. And whether the wind was going to get any stronger.

Suddenly she noticed something on the trunk of one of the trees up ahead. As she drew nearer she saw that someone had carved some kind of symbol into the bark at chest height. It was two Vs, one upside down over the other one to create a diamond in the centre, which had then been hatched in. Each tip of the V sprouted little decorative semi-circles, like swiftly drawn bird wings. There were splodges, like flies that had been swatted with crosses, around the edges.

Stranger still was how the air shimmered more intensely around the symbol. *Almost as if the symbol was somehow generating the shimmer.*

She reached out and touched it – and immediately pulled back her hand. She'd received a weak shock, like the mild electric shock she'd had touching the fence that protected the City Farm's show hens from the urban foxes back in Croydon.

Curiouser and curiouser.

She turned and looked around. Across the faintly misted stretch of shallow water behind her, two plat eyes were coming. Their arms flailed out from their sides as if they were struggling to keep their footing.

'Time to get going...' she muttered, and set off at a jog, splashing through the water. She let the force field take care of keeping her on track, guiding her effortlessly in its own curved, presumably circular, direction. The plat eyes turned and headed after her, making gruff noises to each other that she assumed was communication. She soon lost them in the next swathe of trees.

But whilst she'd given them the slip, there was now something equally scary happening. It was getting dark. *Properly dark.*

She knew she was in real trouble if she had to try and stay out here all night. Wasn't night time when all the scaly things, the snakes and the alligators – *especially the alligators* – did their serious hunting? How would she survive? She certainly couldn't keep on moving, her only hope would be to try and find... what? A tree she could climb? *Could she really spend the night sleeping in a tree?*

She looked up and around at the trees about her, their leaves and branches increasingly indistinct in the enfolding gloom. She thought she could probably scuttle up a trunk – but there were no high, large branches that were big enough for her to lie in. But there was another kind of tree she'd noticed, not a pine tree, one with bigger branches more like the oaks back home. The ones that were often hung with long trails of moss, like true *Swamp Things.* She would have to try and find a batch of them again. It was her only hope.

She came on to a long dry stretch of cotton grass which enabled her to pick up speed, especially as it helped her to see further and more clearly. After a while she came across another symbol, exactly the same as the first. With the failing light she would never have noticed it, but it was carved into a very pronounced, solitary tree stump with a long-fallen, rotten trunk beside it. It was the only significant feature she'd come across for ages. Again the vibration from the field was stronger here. She didn't dare touch it this time.

As she carried on she wondered if she'd missed other, less obvious, makeshift runes along the way. Perhaps it was the symbols, and not the tirtha, that were creating this weird effect?

A sickle moon rose above a new batch of trees, just like the one she'd seen on her first night here. The sky was now more black than blue, and she could see a scattering of tiny stars. She hoped that one of the trees ahead would be good enough to sleep in.

But they were just more of the feathery, piny type, and she was about to start properly panicking when all of a sudden the trees thinned out ahead and when she broke through them she found... *a road!*

It was a pot-holed, dust-and-stone type of road, but nevertheless her heart bounced with joy. This was what she needed! Now she just had to follow it, and surely she would soon come to a town or village or at least a house or petrol station. Or *gas* station, she thought, grinning to herself.

But of course as soon as she joined the road and tried to follow it to the right, in the direction she intuitively wished to go, the invisible field thrust her off it. Frustrated, she pushed herself harder into the air, but was repeatedly and, it had to be said, innocuously, turned away. Finally she ran at it as fast as she could – and was once again running off into the swamp.

She realised that she was going to have to follow the road in the other direction, the one she hadn't felt so much like taking. She felt cross, even crosser for having no one to be cross *with*.

She sent a load of emphatic curses at the night sky as she walked *the wrong way* down the road.

Luckily, it wasn't too hard to see where she was going thanks to the pale light of the moon, which gave a faint shine to the rocky yellow surface of the track. On either side of her there was now very dark woodland, with the occasional odd glimmer of light in its depths, just like on her first night. At one stage she heard ducks quacking somewhere nearby, making a terrible a noise. What a weird time of it she was having, she thought. As if she needed to remind herself. *Still, at least now there was some hope that she wouldn't have to spend the night in a bloody tree.*

After only a few minutes on the road she noticed some sort of blockage up ahead. As she drew nearer she realised that one of the larger trees had fallen over and almost completely blocked it. And then, as she drew nearer still, she suddenly stopped in her tracks, holding her breath. *There was a car under the far side of the tree, its roof partially crushed in!*

The car was a light colour, probably white, but it had a much more modern shape than the one at Cypress House, more like something out of the 1970s cop shows. *Starsky and Hutch* or something. Its lights were off and there was no sound coming from the engine. She wondered if the accident had just happened. Or perhaps it had been there for ages?

What should she do?

Realising that the driver might still be in there – and if he or she was, then they would be injured or worse – she walked around the piled up crown of the tree and approached the car from the passenger side. As soon as she was past the final mass of branches, she crouched down to look inside the smashed out window.

And drew in a deep breath – someone was slumped forward across the steering wheel!

She saw that a large branch had hit the car roof above the driver's head, but it had only partially crumpled down. She would have space to help him out, if the door still worked. Quickly, she ran around to his side and looked in at the broken window. Inside, she noticed that the man was wearing some kind of neat jacket, and that he had wavy, light-coloured hair.

'Hello!' she said, tugging at the metal door handle. 'Are you all right?'

The man lurched up from the wheel and stared into her face. Lizzie screamed, recognising the dull milky look of a plat eye.

For a moment she froze, taking in how different he was to all the rest. The other plat eyes had all had the look of destitution about them, you could tell by their frowns and the sallowness of their skin and the dishevelment of their hair that they'd been through hard times.

But not this one. He was a young white man with thick hair brushed back from his well-groomed, chiselled face. A pair of fine, horn-rimmed spectacles balanced at a slight angle across his nose. And his clothes were smart, a plush looking velvet jacket with an open collar shirt. Only the congealed cut on his forehead – and of course the far-off, cataractous gaze – indicated anything untoward about him.

'Uh,' he coughed. Then his hand thrust through the smashed window at Lizzie's flabbergasted face.

'Ah!' she shrieked, staggering back from his outstretched fingers.

Then he was fumbling for the handle on the inside of the door, and she realised she had to run.

She heard the creaking and crunching of the damaged door as it came open, and the sound of him climbing out of the car.

'Cu... cu...' she heard him calling as she ran.

She was off down the road, well away into the night by the time the plat eye had straightened up and taken a couple of shaky steps toward the rear of the car.

'Cu – come back!' he shouted.

But she didn't hear.

*

God, she'd had enough of running, and enough adrenaline in one day to last a lifetime.

Now it was all she could do to keep putting one foot in front of the other. After another half hour or so, she came to a fork in the road. She examined the track that headed off through the dark trees, but it seemed a lot rougher than the one she was on and in the end she decided to carry on the way she was going. Soon, looking off to her right through the trees, in the direction of the track, she spotted a silver line, broken up by the black criss-cross hatching of branches and foliage. She stopped and scrutinised it for a moment, and then realised that it must be some sort of lake or lagoon.

That didn't seem to offer any more appealing prospect than just carrying on so she... *just carried on.*

And then, what must have been at least another half an hour later, when she was thoroughly exhausted and starting to break into fresh bouts of tears, she finally spotted a broader clearing with *a house* up ahead. She broke into a run, her heart thumping with excitement. There were lights on around the porch. There was a large tree in the centre of the yard, with outhouses. There was a pair of swings on the overgrown lawn.

There was a broken down, old fashioned car in the moonlight.

Her heart sank. She was back.

Back at Cypress House.

Chapter 9: A Revelation

They were emerging from the swamp, through the gangly, moss-strung trees at its edges, the ghost-trees, stumbling across the overgrown lawn, knocking over baby slides and trucks, to come to a halt in front of the house, their ghastly faces turning upward towards her window and she was there, standing, watching, studying them with care as they opened their black, broken-toothed mouths, as the one with the flowing locks and fine jacket and glasses came out from amidst their ranks and in unison with the others, as one, all with one voice, said: 'Help us...' and then she was an alien creature, something else entirely, a creature whose position in the world was as much located through the fabulously rich smell of things as through their appearance – from the warm wine-sweet varnish of wood, the musty old soil rubbed deep into a blanket, the hanging coats above with their subtle odours of... the Mum and her, the Centre... it was Mr Tubs, she realised, she was with him in his dark-bright dream-filled head, his wolves and woods and bracken and true-good-true-evil people sleeping head... And then there was the noise behind, a scraping sound, a chair surely, in the room behind her, in the study, and she turned and walked through into the homely room with its shelves of books, its spirit saturated with learning and knowledge and wisdom and there, at her great-uncle's desk, before the diamond-paned window, was a large, becloaked and hooded figure, and she went forward to ask who it was (she knew really) and when she drew near she saw that the figure was reading her great-uncle's books on the occult, filled with line drawings of knives and animals and robe-draped women and daises and sacrifice and blood, and when she touched the figure's shoulder (she knew who it was) she turned and there she was, her again, *the one she had almost loved, with her long dark hair and wide brow and brown, gentle eyes, and she opened her mouth and said, 'Lizzie...', and Lizzie smiled (she knew there was no point, she was full of hate) and then in the next moment there was the most foul, fanged, swollen, blistered savageness before her and she...*

'Eva!'

She sat bolt upright in bed.

For a while she was completely disorientated. There was darkness above her, a pale half-light defining the objects – the tables and ornaments and weird walls with pictures, birds and plants – all around her. The windows were darkened, but the odours of the room were strong, the soapy fragrance of the un-sweated-on pillow edges, the metallic scent of the silver picture frame beside her, the faint, measly whiff of something acrid, almost alcoholic, like – *a man's aftershave...*

And then, suddenly she remembered where and, more importantly, *who* she was and the scents all vanished.

Lizzie groaned. And groaned.

She realised it must be Monday now, no, *Tuesday*, and everyone at her new school, St Michael's, would know she had disappeared. She imagined the Headteacher, Mr Joseph, talking to Assembly, shoulder to shoulder with plain clothed detectives, camera crews and journalists at the ready. *It is with great sadness that I must tell you that our new pupil, Lizzie Jones, is missing. This is DCI so-and-so, who has come to...*

The news of her disappearance might be on national TV! Everyone would know. *Oh God, her life had imploded.*

She thought back to last night, to reaching the house and banging first on the door and then when there was no response on the living room windows until eventually Lola had let her in. Strangely, like on the first morning, Lola had for a few moments not seemed to recognise her. But as soon as she did she became at first furious with her and then, when Lizzie had once again made a fool of herself by bursting into tears, Lola had taken her upstairs, bathed her and put her to bed. Lizzie hadn't even got to see Caroline, she'd been in such a wretched state.

And now here she was again, back in her adopted bed, after what felt like it had been a long and deep sleep right up until the last few vivid, horrific moments of her dream.

Eva Blane, the Pisaca of Kashi. *She would give anything to forget her.*

Time to get up, get dressed, and go face the music.

*

As she came down the stairs wearing the white dress with roses that Lola had laid out for her, she felt a fire in her belly. She knew that it was time to end all these

91

shenanigans, to finally speak plainly with the headstrong, sickly girl and her carer.

But as soon as she reached the bottom of the stairs she stopped, hearing a door handle click at the opposite end of the hallway, the place she had never been to, Caroline's bedroom. She stood and watched as the door swung outwards and into the hall stepped the tall odd job man and grocer, Mr Paterson.

'Well, hello there,' he called, in a deep baritone voice.

Lizzie flushed. 'Hello,' she said quietly.

'It's our visitor, I've heard about you,' he said, walking down the hall towards her. He was holding a small rectangular black case, like a briefcase. 'Miss Caroline has been telling me.'

'Oh...' She felt disorientated, and didn't know what to say or do. She almost felt like turning round and running back up the stairs. Next thing he was looming above her in his white flat cap, with his wide smile and broad, friendly eyes.

'I'm Mr Paterson,' he said, smiling. 'I'm the one who does anything Lola don't,' he added.

Lizzie nodded. The man was *extremely* tall.

'You look nervous, girl!' he said, laughing. 'Don't worry, I won't eat you!'

She smiled weakly, then said: 'Help me, I need to get out of here.' It was the first thing that came into her head, and as soon as she said it she realised how foolish it sounded.

'Well, there's a storm coming, Hurricane Carla, and we all need to stay put. There'll be no travelling tonight, the nearest town is a hundred klicks away.'

'The road's blocked, how will we even get out when the storm's gone?'

'Blocked, you say? How's that?'

'There's a tree down on it – I saw last night. And there's a crashed car – with a man in it – but he's not a man, he's a plat eye! You know about *them?* What are we going to do about them?'

'My, you have been getting around.' Mr Paterson looked at her appraisingly and then added: 'You don't need to be too scared of them. They're strange all right, but they're only people. People under the spell of Ole Man Hoodoo, who lives on past the lagoon. You stay put and they won't bother you.'

'Ole Man Hoodoo? Who's he?'

'He's been in these parts forever. I run a small farm a couple of klicks away from him, but hardly ever see him. Keeps himself to himself. But I know there are a few people round the bayou who come to him for spells and potions. Mainly the poor folk, wanting stuff to help 'em get rich quick,' he finished, chuckling. 'Or at least to keep the wolf from the door. Whether it works or not, who knows.'

'He can make those poor men obey him?' said Lizzie incredulously. She noticed that one of the man's eyes stared slightly down to the right as he looked at her. He was either *wall-eyed*, as her gran would say, or maybe it was false.

93

'Guess so,' said Mr Paterson. 'I can see you're worried about that. Don't be. Things are... different around here, but don't be overly afraid. Keep your eyes open, stay inside until the storm's blowed over and you'll be safe enough, for sure. I can clear the road and get you out of here after.'

Lizzie felt confused. Half-formed questions and feelings were racing through her mind and it was too hard to focus on any single one. But suddenly she did have a clear idea. 'There's no phone lines, and I need to call home,' she said. 'You don't have a cell phone, do you?'

'I do,' he said. He reached into his pocket and fumbled around whilst Lizzie tried to contain her excitement. Then his hand came out empty. 'Must have left it at home,' he said. 'Hardly ever use it, these days...'

The disappointment must have showed on her face. 'I can bring it with me next time I'm up,' he said.

'Please! Please do, Mr... Mr Paterson, I really need to speak to my mum. I need to tell her... not to worry about me... with the storm...'

'Where did you come from?' he asked, still grinning.

'Didn't Caroline tell you?' *Story, story...*

'Actually, yes, now you say, she did mention something. You're her cousin from England, right? Miss Elizabeth?'

'Yes,' said Lizzie, relieved.

'How long are you over here for, Miss E.?'

'Just a few days... then my mum's coming back to collect me...'

94

'You off back to England then?'

'Yes. After we've been to New Orleans for a couple of nights.'

'Righty-ho. Well, you just make yourself comfortable, settle down for a night or two. This storm's gonna be a howler, for sure. I'll be just down the road, through the woods, nearby the lake, if you need me. And I've brought up some lovely fig jam as a treat...'

'OK,' said Lizzie, in a small voice.

He stared at her intensely for a moment and she felt herself go increasingly red.

'Don't you worry, Miss Elizabeth,' he said, then gave her cheek a quick pinch and turned and walked into the nearest doorway, the kitchen. She heard the back door open and slam shut.

Lizzie stood frozen for a moment, her cheek burning where he'd pinched it.

Who was he? *What had he been doing in Caroline's room?*

Despite everything he'd said, and his relaxed, friendly style, something didn't ring true about Mr Paterson. Suddenly, she felt a whole lot less confident.

*

When she was sure he wasn't coming back, Lizzie went into the kitchen and hurried up to the back door with its glazed half window. She was studying it when she heard someone clear their throat behind her.

She spun round and Lola was there.

'How come when he goes out you're not panicking about the wards?' said Lizzie.

She wished she was better at reading body language as Lola went silently over to the hob and picked up a metal pitcher. She was scowling, sullen, certainly – but was there something else there? Embarrassment – *or shame?*

'And who is Ole Man Hoodoo?'

Lola glanced across at her, with a strangely insolent look for an adult. 'Who?' she said, filling the pitcher from the tap.

'Ole Man Hoodoo. That man – Mr Paterson – was talking about him. Says he lives down by the lake. Says he's the one who's made all these people into plat eyes.'

'Lots of strange folk round here,' said Lola. 'You best keep yourself to yourself.'

'But don't you think we need to do something? He can't be allowed to put spells on other people, and leave them wandering around all day and night in the swamp. There are alligators and snakes out there, they might get killed.'

'It's none of my business. I just keep 'em away from this house, that's what I do. Keep Miss Caroline safe.'

'So why aren't you fixing the ward on the kitchen door now he's gone out through it?'

Water splashed out the spout of the kettle as Lola spun round at her. 'You ask too many questions for a young girl! You'd think you'd be grateful we'd taken you in an' looked after you!'

Lizzie took a small step backwards, realising she'd pushed the woman far enough. It was a shame, she wanted to push further – there was so many inconsistencies in everyone's stories – but she would have to wait and find another moment.

'OK,' she said. 'And thanks – for looking after me, especially last night.'

'That's fine, child,' said Lola, looking down.

∗

After pecking away at the toast and fruit on the breakfast table, Lizzie finally decided to break the silence.

'You know, I'd really like to be your friend,' she said. Corny, but there you go. *She needed to try a new approach.*

Caroline had been half-heartedly scraping her usual piece of melon away from its rind. She stopped and looked across the table at Lizzie. Then, after a few moments of staring at her, she looked back down at the melon and continued digging at it with her spoon.

'How about no more hard questions? We just talk about normal things,' said Lizzie.

'Like what?'

'I don't know. Like the sort of things girls talk about. Like...' The first thing that came into her mind was horses, but looking at the wheelchair she checked herself. 'Films? Music?'

Caroline's pale eyebrows arched with each suggestion. She remained staring steadfastly at her breakfast plate.

'Boys?'

Caroline frowned intensely. Lizzie guessed she was too young – or too sheltered. She realised she should have suggested books and was about to bring them up when Caroline said:

'Have you got a boyfriend?'

'Um, no,' said Lizzie, feeling wrong-footed. She flushed.

'Anyone you like?'

'Like? Yes, sure, of course there's people I like...'

'Who?'

This wasn't going how she'd planned. 'Well, there's... there's... there's this Indian boy who's very... nice.'

'What's his name?'

'He's called Pandu.'

'Funny name.'

Lizzie shrugged.

'How do you know him?'

'It's a long story.'

'Tell me.'

She needed to... *redirect* this now.

'He goes to the same school as me,' she said. 'We're just friends. How about you? Do you like any... *guys?*' She felt pleased with herself, sure the Americanism would help divert the subject away from her.

'That's not a long story,' said Caroline.

'There's always someone,' said Lizzie.

They were silent again for a while, then Lizzie added:

'Hey, we're all keeping our little secrets, here.'

Caroline set down her spoon – having eaten literally nothing – and said:

'No, I don't – like any *"guys"*. I never get to meet anyone out here. And anyway, if I did, why would they like a cripple like me?'

'Don't use that word!'

'Why not?'

'It's terrible.'

'But it's true.'

'You might be in a wheelchair – but that doesn't mean someone won't find you attractive...'

Caroline raised her eyebrows again.

'You are – you are very pretty,' said Lizzie.

'Thanks.'

'You are.'

'Like I said. Thanks.'

That didn't go so well. OK, she may as well go back to the harder line.

'Look,' she said, 'we both know that there's something really weird going on here.'

Caroline glared at her breakfast.

'With all those creatures out there we need to try and find a way out of this place – or at least a way to get rid of them. I'm wracking my brains, but it would really help me if I could just talk to you – without raising your hackles.'

'Lovely way of putting it,' said Caroline.

Lizzie took that as consent for her to carry on.

'So, can I ask you a few more things about yourself?'

A small nod, still looking down. Lizzie noticed her pull Sally Ally closer into her side.

'OK, great. Just tell me when you don't want to answer or go on – I promise I'll stop.'

No nod this time, but Lizzie felt the assent. She was starting to feel like some cop in a show. *OK, time to stop the Americanisms.*

'You really do love that doll, don't you?'

Again silence, but the wooden doll received an extra squeeze. Lizzie spotted the strange snake hanging out of Sally Ally's mouth again and had to stop herself from wrinkling up her nose.

'Ignoring the fact you should never ask a girl her age - how old are you?' she said.

Caroline looked up and held Lizzie's eye. 'Eleven.'

Like Lola had said. 'And what were your mum and dad's names?'

'Julie and Charles.'

'Did your dad ever talk about his relatives?'

'Not really.'

'Do you know if he had any English relatives?'

'Yes. Because he *was* English.'

'Oh, right. And do you know any of his relatives?'

'Yes, his sister – my aunt.'

'What was her name?' said Lizzie, taking a sip of juice.

'Evelyn.'

Lizzie coughed on her juice.

'Evelyn?'

'Yes, Evelyn. What's so strange about that?'

Everything, Lizzie thought. She must be getting something wrong. Evelyn had died over twenty years

100

ago, she had seen her grave in the garden. Either it was some other Evelyn or... *or what?*

'Do you know her surname?'

'Yes, Hartley.'

Despite the heat, Lizzie felt her skin begin to crawl. Evelyn Hartley. It was the same name. *There couldn't be more than one.*

The room suddenly felt like it was sliding about, the corners tilting and the roof coming down at the edges. One thought loomed large in Lizzie's head: Time. *The tirthas can play with time as well as space.* The preposterous idea she'd had the day before, which had been nothing more than an absurd joke to herself, might actually be true.

'Are you OK?'

She realised she had been staring vacantly into space. 'Yes,' she said, struggling to pull herself together. 'Yes, I'm fine.' *Questions. Keep asking questions.* Hurriedly she said:

'You said something strange to me about your dad – that he was a coward. How come?'

'He was a deserter from the war. He was in England, but he came over here to escape being called up.'

'You were born in England, then?'

'No.'

'So how did you find out?'

'My grandfather told me. That was why my aunt never saw him again.'

'So, he escaped from, let's get this right...the Second World War... to...'

'No,' said Caroline, her lip curling, 'the First World War! Papa was very old when he had me. He was in his sixties.'

So that was it, confirmed. The tirtha must have sent her back in time. Everything felt like it was crumbling inside her.

'But... and...' she began.

'You sure you're OK?'

'Every day starts exactly the same. The weather, it's always the same, warm in the morning, baking by lunch, then clouding over later... the winds in the evening with the storm, but then... the hurricane. It never arrives...'

Caroline was staring fixedly at her.

'No one ever eats. Everyone forgets things. What's kept locked in the desk in the room beside mine? And... who is that strange man?'

'I don't know where you're going with all this,' said Caroline. 'But to answer your questions – the weather here is often very repetitive, this heat plays havoc with your appetite and memory, the desk just has some old things of my father's and – and the man is a local farmer who brings us groceries and fixes things round the house. The things that Lola can't fix.'

'What was he doing in your room?'

A moment's silence. 'He was giving me some medicine.'

'Medicine?'

'Yes – just some stuff for my disease.'

'Oh.'

'You *sure* you're all right?'

102

'Mm.'

'Why don't you go and have a lie down? I think you might have caught something out on the swamp yesterday.'

'Maybe that's a good idea.'

She stood up and began to walk out of the room.

'Lizzie.'

It was the first time Caroline had used her name. She stopped and looked around at her.

'I can feel it too. I can't put my finger on it, but I know there is something strange going on here. More than just the plat eyes. But everything will be OK – just as soon as my brother gets back.'

Lizzie drew in a sharp breath. 'OK,' she said, quietly.

The last thing she could do now was tell Caroline what had happened to her brother.

Chapter 10: The Broken Temple

There had been a temple there at the sacred kund on the Ganges for nearly two thousand years, from the very origins of Brahmism. And there had been worship there even before that.

The long-disused temple of Brahma with its hidden magic had been built and rebuilt. It had started as little more than a pile of stones, mounted up around a sacred spring. Successive holy men had sought it out and constructed ever more elaborate structures, of mud, wood, stone, brick and mortar over the eons. At some stage, one, lost in time, had correctly identified the exact location of the tirtha and ordered a bespoke portal be created with an image of the Lord of Creation and his sacred mount depicted upon it. Whether he had ever shared the secret, or knew the origins of its power, no one knows, or will know.

The temple had seen rulers and empires come and go across the ancient city – the mahajanapadas, Mauryans, Guptas, the Mughals and the British. It had absorbed the daily acts of puja of countless saddhus as well as ordinary folk. And always it had stayed the same, steadfastly watching out over the swirling waters of the holy Ganges.

Until now. It was a young mother, clutching her new-born babe, who was the first to hear it. Standing on the ghat, her immediate thought when she heard the dull rumbling was that the hazy, sunny weather was a deception and that a storm had developed to the west, unseen. But as she looked around what she saw left her crying out to Lord Shiva.

The ancient temple was collapsing into the river!

At first it seemed to go slowly, a crack like a crooked grin beginning to show in its stone work level with the ghat. But then there was a massive crunching, and a grinding noise – a noise like the end of days – and the upper half of the temple tumbled forward into the water.

The woman screamed, worried of omens. She went running to the nearest saddhu.

Quickly, the dust settled. All that remained was a broken set of steps leading down to a flooded chamber, a squat well and, at chest height in the bankside wall, a niche now exposed to the elements.

A niche with a primitive sketch of four-faced Brahma and the *hamsa*, his sacred goose.

*

The Kali priestess Lamya arrived at the temple shortly after its collapse.

Dressed in non-religious garb, including jeans and a grey long sleeve shirt, she cursed aloud as soon as she saw the damage. *How was she going to put the plan into action if the tirtha had been destroyed?* Feeling rising panic, she hurried down the last few ghats to examine the wreckage.

Miraculously, the tirtha seemed to have survived, embedded as was now evident within a section of the clayey riverbank. Examining the damage, she saw that the ledge that ran around the outer temple wall to the entrance above the river was still intact. Whilst the entrance itself and the first few steps leading down into the temple were now little more than a heap of rubble parting the swirling river, the bottom section of steps still seemed usable. She realised she could make her way around the ledge and jump on to these remaining steps, then leap into the tirtha and pray it still worked.

The only problem she could see was the young man in the neat blue suit who was standing gawping down into the vault, first on the scene.

Looking down the ghat, Lamya quickly surveyed the other people in the vicinity. There was the mother with her baby, talking fifty metres away to a bewildered priest. Then beyond them were a few more people, starting to run towards the scene. *Nothing would be clear to them.* So, it was just the sharply dressed businessman.

She jumped down the three small ghats towards him. He looked up – a handsome face, clean shaven, with fetching hazel eyes – just in time to see her sickle knife come swiping from her belt towards his face. But he didn't feel it strike his cheek or mouth and thought for a moment he must have imagined it, the young woman looking into his eyes seemed so bright and pretty, how could she have wielded a knife at him? And then he noticed the fine spray of red splashing on her top, little spurts of it coming from... *him*... and then he reached up and felt the split in the skin across his neck and surely no, surely this couldn't be it, no...*in his mind's eye the snaking blue river of Mother Ganga pouring down from Lord Shiva's lustrous hair...*

Lamya shoved his dead body into the vault where it landed with a dull thud. She looked up. No one seemed to have seen that, she was in luck! *She couldn't risk anyone seeing her using the portal, if it still worked.* She jumped on to the ledge, ran around it with the dexterity of a mountain goat, and dropped down on to the steps. Within moments she was in the exposed cellar and, after quickly cleaning her blade on his suit, with surprising strength – the product of nothing more supernatural than her astonishing willpower – she lifted the young man's corpse and tipped it into the well. Then she stepped up to the wall with the inset niche and the picture of Brahma.

'Kali Ma, overseer of infinite permutations, guide me now!'

And, grabbing hold of the bottom edge of the niche, she hoisted herself up into it, and disappeared.

*

Soon after, Pandu and Inspector Raj Faruwallah, who had been following the priestess with the burly Sergeant Singh at a discreet distance higher up on the ghat, were down in the broken temple.

'She must have dumped him in the kund!' said Pandu, glancing down into the black hole.

'No time for that,' said Raj. 'If we're going to catch her, we need to go through now.'

'Yes, Uncle,' said Pandu. Inside, he seethed with unspeakable anger and a vile hatred for the priestess.

'Singh – cordon everybody back – now!' Raj shouted, looking up at the Sikh sergeant who stood above them, gun in hand.

'Quickly, everybody back! Move away from the building – it could be dangerous,' shouted the big, bearded man. Within moments, Raj and Pandu could no longer see any of the half dozen or so faces that had begun peering eagerly over the broken temple walls at them.

'OK, I'll go...' began Raj, but he was too late – Pandu had already leapt in, and vanished.

The Inspector pulled himself up, thrust himself face-first at the stone image, and next moment was gone.

*

Lizzie lay on her back, staring up at the linen canopy of the four poster bed. The afternoon heat was humid and stifling. She had opened the windows and closed the shutters, casting everything in deep shade. She was stuck in a time warp on the other side of the world with a shrewish girl and her maid, surrounded by zombies, their only visitor a vaguely disturbing odd job man from down by the lake.

She wanted to give up, to let herself submerge into the cool, dark, remote waters of her despair. A place she would enter and never have to leave. A place where she could abnegate all responsibility for decisions, for her whole dumbass life. *But there was a fly in the room that was driving her nuts.*

Every time it landed and a period of quiet ensued she would try and forget about it. But then, no matter how hard she hoped, it would start up its low-pitched buzz right in the very core of her brain again. On every third or fourth flight it would for added effect come and circle the bed canopy a few times. Once it even bumped into the side of her head and she caught the unpleasant wing-and-hairiness of it on the edge of her hand as it bombed away.

It was no good. *She was going to have to do something.*

With the battle call of a Nippon warrior she leapt from the maudlin zone of her bed, wielding a rolled up copy of *Life* magazine like a Samurai sword. A couple of complete misses made her realise she would need to open the shutters again.

As soon as she did so and looked back around the room the fly had gone, evidently deftly swooping around her clumsy figure to disappear into the freedom of the fresh – *fresher* – air outside.

She put the magazine down on the dresser, feeling foolish but relieved. She knew then that she had to do something, it just wasn't in her nature to give up.

So what next?

As she looked around, reflecting, she spotted the smaller door again. *The bureau.* She would get it open, no matter what.

She looked around for something to use to force it open. There was a comb, aftershave, china trinkets, a couple of small decorative bowls containing cuff links and pins. Nothing that seemed up to the job. She opened the dresser draws, but they were full of socks and pants, she didn't want to riffle through them.

She went and opened the little door and stepped into the room. She decided to check again the small drawers below the fold-up desk. Pulling them open, she rummaged through the odd notes and scraps of paper, pencils and pens, finding a rubber and a pencil sharpener and... *a letter opener.*

She picked it out and examined it. It had a serrated silver blade and ivory handle, yellowed with age. It looked expensive. *It would do.*

With the fingertips of one hand, she pulled the desk a fraction away from the unit and managed to jam the tip of the letter opener in, just to the side of the small keyhole. Then she pulled the wedged letter opener towards her, at the same time pulling back as hard as she could with her fingertips.

There was a snapping sound, the letter opener broke in two, and the bureau sprang open and banged against her hip.

She pulled out the two support panels and rested it on them, but from her initial, cursory glance she had already surmised the truth.

The bureau was empty.

'What are you doin'!'

Lizzie spun round to see Lola standing in the doorway.

'I...I...' began Lizzie. She'd seen her angry before, but never quite as angry as this. She was shaking all over and her hands kept moving up to her eyes and cheeks. Her mouth was open in a distorted grimace.

'You were doin' things you oughtn't'!' shouted Lola. 'Again! You're a naughty little girl! You don't have no respect!'

She advanced quickly on Lizzie who backed up between the desk and the window in fear.

'I'm sorry,' said Lizzie.

'Sorry's no good! You got to stop meddlin'! Look, you've broken the nice bureau now...' Small bits of spit flew from Lola's mouth.

Lizzie looked at the small lock, which had broken off, and the splintered edge of the desk where she'd levered it.

'There's nothing in there,' she said.

'Hmm!' Again Lizzie sensed something in Lola's expression that she wished she could pinpoint. Something alongside the anger. *Remorse?* Something definitely a little... *sheepish.*

'I don't want you causin' no more trouble, I've had enough,' Lola declared. 'You can stay in your room for the rest of the day!' She lifted the desk up and tried in vain to re-fix the little lock, muttering curses under her breath.

'Gonna have to see if *he* can fix it,' she said.

Lizzie was about to say sorry again but held back. Instead she just watched in silence as Lola fumbled with the broken desk.

Eventually the woman turned and said to her: 'You don't tell Miss Caroline nothin' about this, OK? She's got enough on her plate, without havin' to worry that you've been breaking her poor dead daddy's things too!'

Lizzie glanced up into her large brown eyes. 'OK,' she said. 'Sorry.'

'Hm!' snorted Lola and turned and left the room.

Lizzie heard her slam the bedroom door. Her misery at having made Lola angry soon disappeared as she began to wonder... to wonder – wonder what?

To wonder what she'd been hiding.

*

In the end, Lizzie stayed put in her room most of the afternoon.

With the heat and all that had happened in the last few days she needed to rest and take her mind off things, at least for a short while, so she decided to do some reading. She quickly skimmed the pristine copy of *Life* magazine, dated August 25th, 1961, with its dreary black and white photos of people in Berlin, and then noticed a small row of books in an antique bookshelf near the door. In amongst them, she found a little hardback copy of *Alice in Wonderland* with lovely drawings, and she began to re-read it. It was one of her favourites, a book that her great-uncle Eric had sent her many, many years ago, in what she now knew was an act of preparing her for the fact that mystical realms really did exist down the rabbit hole, behind the wardrobe, at the bottom of the garden...

In another moment down went Alice after it, never once considering how in the world she was to get out again.

Exactly.

She could write her own version, *Lizzie in Zombieland.*

She wished that she had met her great-uncle when she was older. Why couldn't her mum have taken her down to see him – at least once? She was sure he would have given her insights, things to go on, *something* to help her make more sense of all this. She supposed that's one reason why he had at least written a diary. *If only he'd done it like everyone else, i.e. on a laptop, then at least she and Ashlyn could have searched it for key information as opposed to combing literally thousands of pages written out in his illegible scrawl.*

She surprised herself, finishing the book in one sitting. Afterwards, she went downstairs and ate another hamster-sized meal with Caroline – she was sure now that the heat and slow, warped nature of time in the house was reducing all their appetites to virtually nought – and then sat with her in the living room. When they talked, they kept the subject away from anything controversial. Caroline told Lizzie about the books she loved, which Lizzie found surprisingly advanced, including lots of classics and particularly Jane Austen. Surprisingly, *Northanger Abbey* was her favourite, not one of the big romances like *Pride and Prejudice.*

Then, around half past nine, after Lola had sullenly brought them both a drink, as the winds banged the shutters in gusts, they both retired to their beds.

All a bit... *Northanger Abbey* itself, thought Lizzie. *With zombies, of course.*

Chapter 11: Through the Keyhole

In the pale, English afternoon sunlight, Lord Nataraja glowed silver-bronze and danced, with no sign of effort, on Apasmara, the demon of ignorance and fear.

All was perfectly still in the Indian Garden, one of the nearly two dozen garden rooms delineated by hedges, streams, ponds and outhouses that made up the Rowan Cottage garden, a garden which was itself set amidst the sprawling ancient oaks of Hoad's Wood, deep within the Herefordshire countryside.

A small bird, brown, nothing more extraordinary than a sparrow, came down in a flick of wings and took hold of the topmost edge of the Lord of Dance's ring of fire, the flaming circle that represented the manifest cosmos. The sparrow perched there, darting glances at upper sections of the dark, surrounding hedges. After a moment, it clearly decided there was nothing for it here, and left the garden in a burst of energy and feather.

Silence reigned again. The statue stared noncommittally at the showy pink flowers of the rhododendron bush, straight ahead of it.

And then something that shouldn't happen happened.

In the mild, empty spring air, near the feet of the defeated dwarf, first a foot in a leather sandal, then a leg, legs in blue jeans, then a torso, arm, arms in a grey top, and finally a face, small and round, pretty, with short black hair, became real, and a whole woman was stumbling to catch herself against the Lord's aureole of bronze flame.

As soon as she had steadied herself, the woman glanced all around like the sparrow, and then hurried off past the rhododendron and out of the Indian garden.

Nataraja held his pose.

Moments later, two more figures materialised beside him, first a gangly Indian youth in grey trousers and a white shirt, and then a portly young man with a fine moustache, dressed in a dun-coloured uniform.

Without a word, both immediately set off in the same direction as the woman, heading down a hedge-lined corridor that led into a semi-circular garden at the rear of Rowan Cottage. There, wasting no time, they ran past the sundial in the middle of the lawn and then down along the side of the house and out on to the front drive, where they were just in time to hear the woman's feet crunching away up the gravel drive, towards the road.

'Lizzie?' said Pandu.

'No,' said Raj. 'No time. We have to follow her now or we'll lose her.'

'OK,' said Pandu.

They both ran off in pursuit of the priestess.

As their shoes slapped away on the drive, the old front door of the cottage opened and a brown-haired woman dressed in jeans and a check shirt came out. She walked forward and looked down the drive.

Rachel Jones was sure she'd heard someone outside, and had thought it might be Godwin arriving – but seeing no one, she shrugged and walked back into the house.

*

'Where am I?' Lizzie thought, opening her eyes and staring up at the strange four poster bed. Her mind raced in panic.

It was a few seconds before she remembered Lola, and then she gradually began to recall all the horrendous details of the last three days. Her sense of alarm declined, although it refused to go altogether. *Like a nasty black cat shooed away but still sitting in a corner of her mind, waiting for the right moment to return.*

She got up, dressed, and then headed down the landing towards the stairs. She was standing at the top, just about to descend when the white-capped figure of Mr Paterson walked past in the hallway below, heading towards Caroline's room. He was carrying the small black case he'd had with him the day before.

She froze. With her heart thumping, she waited until she'd heard him give a little knock, open the door, and shut it again after going in.

What was he up to? All kinds of dark thoughts and images rushed through her head.

She had to do something. She had to check Caroline was OK. It was her duty. But...

She was scared.

Not just scared – petrified. She didn't know why, but she knew – *knew* – he was up to no good. She'd been through so much, she could just sense these things by now.

An image of Eva flashed in her mind. She realised that, for her, there were two Eva's: the terrible, treacherous one, who had betrayed her trust more than anyone else in the world ever, the one whose image was now indelibly fixed as the monstrous Pisaca with her swollen features and revolting fangs – and then the handsome, dark-haired Polish woman who had been so helpful and kind and reassuring when Lizzie most needed her. They both existed side by side and sometimes in her dreams or moments of forgetfulness she would feel herself starting to smile when she thought about the good Eva. *But only for a moment.*

And... the thing was, Mr Paterson somehow with his kind eyes and ever-present grin reminded her of the *good* Eva.

As soon as she thought that her legs turned to jelly.

What if Mr Paterson was a demon too?

She physically shook herself, to get some sense back. She had no reason – *absolutely no reason* – to think that. To go scaring the heebie-jeebies out of herself, as her gran would say.

OK. Be calm.

She would go and check.

But the feeling of jelliness in her legs didn't go as she crept down the stairs and then along the hallway towards Caroline's bedroom, in fact it began to spread into her belly and then up into her arms. It even felt like her brain was getting wobbly, as she pressed her ear up against the door.

'Yes, there we go now, just pop those in your mouth and it'll help ease the pain...' she heard Mr Paterson say. Lizzie dropped to her knees and peered in through the keyhole.

Caroline's bed was directly opposite the door so Lizzie had a good view of her. The tall man was standing beside the girl as she lay there, her blonde hair splayed out around her on the pillow. Her raggedy doll, Sally Ally, was as ever clutched tightly to her side. As Lizzie watched, Caroline lifted her hand up to her mouth and swallowed what Lizzie guessed must be a pill. She screwed her eyes up and said:

'These are so bitter,' in a dispirited voice.

'There, there, they'll do you a lot of good. Help keep that nasty illness in check,' said Mr Paterson. He turned to the bottom of the bed, where he had already opened his small black case.

After rummaging around in it, he suddenly turned back to Caroline and Lizzie gasped, spotting a large syringe in his hand.

'Do we have to?' said Caroline hollowly.

'Yes, child, you know you do.'

Lizzie felt disbelief as she saw the big man lean over and the pale girl offer him her forearm. Lizzie winced as the large needle went in, and Mr Paterson drew back the plunger. Bright red blood began to fill the tube.

'Oh my God...' Lizzie muttered.

'Just a little more,' said Mr Paterson, but Caroline had already turned her head away on the pillow and Lizzie was unsure if she was even conscious.

'There we go,' he said finally, pulling the needle out. He turned back to his case and brought out a small plastic cup. Then he squirted some of the blood into the cup and, to Lizzie's horror and disgust, drank it.

'Ahh!' he said, smiling and wiping his mouth with his sleeve. 'Just a little to keep me going!'

He drained the rest of the blood into a tube which he stopped up and replaced in his bag.

Lizzie felt a wave of incredulity, followed by terror and panic, sweep over her. She was right! He was a demon! Or if not a demon, someone – or *something* – equally horrific...

In the next moment Mr Paterson did something equally strange and grotesque. He reached over the bed and brushed the back of his hand over Caroline's brow – the young girl was clearly asleep now – then lifted her doll from the cradle of her arm. For the first time Lizzie noticed that the doll was wearing a kind of kilt or dress and small boots, and that it had white zigzags painted up its brown chest. It didn't actually look like a doll at all, she thought fleetingly. *More like a crazy shaman.* Then

120

Mr Paterson raised Sally Ally up and pressed her against his cheek.

Lizzie watched wide-eyed as the grown man who had just drank a child's blood proceeded to stroke and cuddle that same girl's doll adoringly. *And she thought she'd seen it all.*

'Mm, perhaps the most important painted stick in the whole wide world,' he said with his eyes shut, smiling. And then his next words sent a chill through Lizzie's whole body: 'Eva will be so pleased to have you, my precious little Artefact. However will she reward me?'

Fear flooded Lizzie's mind. Did he just say *Eva?* The Pisaca was dead, wasn't she? Lizzie and Pandu and the others had all watched as she'd been zapped away in some kind of vortex after catching the Lingam in her bare hands. What possible connection could Eva have had with this man? *She must have misheard him.*

Lizzie tried to ignore her thumping heart, and concentrated back on the moment. Was Caroline OK? Maybe she wasn't sleeping, maybe she was unconscious – or worse? *Where was Lola when they needed her?*

Suddenly her feelings of terror multiplied as Mr Paterson replaced Sally Ally in bed with Caroline and began to shut his bag. He was coming out!

As quickly and as quietly as she could she scooted down the corridor towards the stairs. If she was really fast she could be back up them before he opened the door.

And then, just as she reached the bottom of the staircase she heard the door open and slam behind her.

She couldn't help but look round.

Mr Paterson stood slightly stooped, briefcase in hand, staring at her from the end of the hallway.

She stared back at him, the horror written large across her face.

Then, after a few moments, she realised that he wasn't going to speak to her. He was just going to... *stare* at her.

She felt her knees buckle, grabbed the banister just in time to stop herself from falling down. She had never felt so scared in all her life. Even when she was running away from the Pisaca, when at least the adrenalin had kicked in.

Mr Paterson began to walk down the corridor towards her. He continued to look at her, but the expression on his face was inscrutable.

Suddenly, her survival instincts kicked in and, without a word, she scrambled backwards up the stairs. She was halfway up when he came past the bottom of the staircase.

He glanced briefly up at her with a half smile. And then was gone into the kitchen.

Lizzie might never have been so scared in all her life but in the next moment she was back down the stairs and edging herself up against the frame of the open kitchen door.

'...watch that young lady, now...' he was saying.

'Yes I will. She was breakin' into the desk just yesterday mornin',' came Lola's response.

'The desk? Does she know anything about the Book?'

'No, I don't think so...' There was something about Lola's voice, a quavering tone that wasn't normally there. *As if she was scared too.*

'OK, well it don't matter. Everything's happening today, there's gonna be one hell of a change taking place later, just you wait and see!' Mr Paterson laughed sharply, and Lizzie heard the back door open.

Her courage astounded even herself sometimes. She burst into the kitchen and saw Lola stooped over the sink, one hand on her head. Without saying anything, Lizzie ran past her and up to the back door. Mr Paterson was in the yard, opening the door of his yellow pickup truck. He climbed up into the cabin.

'Wai... no! Miss Lizzie!' Lola cried, emerging from her fug, as Lizzie darted out through the back door and across the dusty courtyard to the back of the truck.

There was a harsh metallic grinding sound as Mr Paterson turned the key in the ignition, and the truck shook into life. Lizzie caught a whiff of the diesel fumes as she grabbed hold of the back of the truck and pulled herself up into it.

In the back of the pickup there were several crates full of vegetables, a couple of spades, a fork, and a tarpaulin crumpled up on one side. Lizzie quickly slid herself under the tarpaulin.

The truck lurched off down the lane.

Chapter 12: Removing the Glyphs

Thomas Bennett was bored.

Bored, bored, bored, bored, bored.

It was Hebley itself that was boring, he thought, as the light began to fade and he sauntered slowly home up the main street, hands in pockets. Why did his dad have to be a farmer? *Why couldn't they live somewhere more interesting, with more to do?* Hereford for instance, or even Ludlow would do.

He looked around at the familiar sights. The Spar, the green with its duck pond, the old wooden bus shelter, the deli and pub, the 'Craven Crow' bookshop owned by that old bat of a witch, Madeline Kendall. What was there to do here? Even the nearby playground, with its 'natural play' sawn-up trees and tunnels was dull.

He looked in the window of the deli at various heaps of green, grey, and black olives, and sighed. There was a white Scottie tied up outside the shop, which reminded him of the dog that his mum had looked after when Old Man Hartley died. *Mr Tubs.* What a stupid name for a dog.

Then he remembered the *new* girl, Lizzie Jones, the one who'd inherited the mutt and Rowan Cottage and who wasn't so new anymore. With her links to the village witches she was a weird one all right, but she was also... *interesting.* He almost wanted to censor his own thoughts as soon as that word popped up in them. But he couldn't deny it. She *was* interesting. Independent. He liked that in a person.

After his mum had handed Mr Tubs over to Lizzie and her mum, Thomas had had only the one proper contact with Lizzie in the field, last November when they saw the hunt go by. He'd seen her around in their school, but he was in a different class and they had studiously ignored one another as they passed in corridors or the playground or the street. Or, he hated to admit it to himself, *she* had rather ignored *him*. Maybe he'd been too hard on her in that field? He didn't think he had, couldn't really remember what he'd said – but he knew she'd been upset by the hunt (*girls!*), and perhaps he could have been just a little more understanding. *Perhaps.*

Oh, look at him now, he was even thinking like a girl! *Understanding...*

But he decided that, next time he saw her, he would say something to her. Invite her out for a bike ride. Or something.

Would she like a bike ride...?

He was stewing on it, wondering what else he might suggest if he saw her, when he noticed a woman heading down the other side of the street past the Spar.

She was dark skinned and she had short hair and was wearing jeans and a nice top and... she was quite fit, he had to admit. What was she up to in Hebley? He thought briefly of the Feral Child last year, the one who everyone had been talking about living wild in the woods, but who had gone off the radar quite quickly. He'd always suspected the Feral Child was a gypo kid (*can't say gypo anymore, watch yourself Thomas*), but no one had ever found out. Was the woman disappearing down the street a gypsy? He didn't think so, she looked too moneyed. *And she really was quite fit.*

As he turned to carry on up the street he stopped suddenly, confronted by two more *Asian-looking* types, coming right up in front of him. One was a stringy teenage boy, wearing filthy old sandals and a loose shirt and the other was a short, stocky man with wavy hair, wearing a uniform like a soldier.

When the two saw him looking at them they seemed to change their demeanour, to slow down a bit, stroll instead of stride. With his left arm strangely rigid at his side, the man looked in at the books on display in The Craven Crow and said to his companion:

'Hmm, lovely old bookshop, eh, son?'

'Yes – Dad,' replied the teenager, somewhat reluctantly.

The man looked round at Thomas and gave him a warm smile. 'Wonderful weather for this time of year, isn't it?' he said.

Thomas looked at him blankly. *What was wrong with his arm?*

The man looked at the boy for a few more seconds then, realising no reply was coming, smiled at him again and walked past with the youth – who didn't look anywhere near young enough to be his son.

'Bloody *tourists*,' Thomas muttered, staring after them as they headed down towards the church and Lady Blane's house, following the woman at a distance.

He wondered why the man had moved his arm behind his body now.

*

'Damn! She's gone...'

Having to slow down so that the village boy didn't suspect anything – and do his best to cover up his gun with his arm – meant that Raj had lost sight of the Kali priestess.

'She was heading down that lane, towards the church,' said Pandu.

'She wouldn't go in there, surely?' said Raj, as they headed along the gravel road. On the right was a large house set within a lovely garden and on the left was a high brick wall with gates into an even larger house, with tall chimneys on a roof that sloped right down to an overgrown lawn. This house had worn timber beams set into the walls, which were covered by abundant ivy and pink roses. The gates to the house were shut, and there were no vehicles in the drive.

The two Indians walked to the end of the lane and passed through a wooden kissing gate, which had a small arch carved with angels blowing trumpets. A stone path led up to the church door, with mown paths leading away either side through the graveyard.

'No, I can't imagine she'd go in the church,' said the Inspector, stroking his chin. He looked left and right, checking the paths that circled the church.

'Over there,' he said, pointing.

Pandu followed Raj as the Inspector strode off towards a small gate set in a wall shared between the graveyard and the large house.

'It's open,' said Pandu as they came up to it. He pushed the gate open a little further and peered round the edge.

A small, sandstone path led up to a lily pond with a statue of a naked boy in the middle. The flower beds on either side of the path were overgrown with giant, thistle like plants, threaded through with roses and honeysuckle gone wild. Beyond the pond the path carried on until a few steps led down to a sunken patio area at the rear of the beautiful old house.

'No sign of her,' he whispered.

Raj peered round his shoulder.

'Doesn't look like anyone's been taking care of this place for quite a while,' he said. 'Let's go take a look.'

They entered the garden and Pandu pushed the gate to. They walked down past the pond, checking the house windows for any sign of activity. The sky above the house was turning grey as night began to fall.

'What do we say if someone comes out?' said Pandu.

'Come to read the meter,' said Raj.

But no one appeared and the house remained silent as they reached the patio.

'Probably away on holiday,' said Pandu.

'Yes, but people with this much money at least have a gardener...'

They walked along the back of the house, sheltering their eyes from the reflection as they checked the sumptuous, empty rooms within. Raj was the first to reach the back door and, without a word, he tried the handle.

The door opened. The Inspector and boy looked at one another.

Raj nodded, and they went in.

*

The only thing keeping Lizzie from getting out and jumping off the back of the moving truck was her conviction that she had to do this to get out of this place. *To get home.* She knew that somehow, Mr Paterson held the key.

Why did he drink Caroline's blood? she wondered, her cheek pressed uncomfortably into the bumping, gritty, grooved metal floor of the pickup. Wasn't that why Eva had been killing all those street children in Kashi? *To feed off their blood, and keep herself alive.*

And... had Mr Paterson really mentioned Eva's name? *Perhaps he was a demon too, and he somehow knew the Pisaca through the tirthas?* Maybe he didn't know she was dead, it had only been a few months ago. Whatever, Lizzie felt a petrifying numbness creep through her just at the thought of there being some connection between the two of them. *She must have misheard him.* She had to believe that. *At least for now,* said a little voice inside her head.

As the truck bounced around she thought more about Mr Paterson and Caroline. How long had he been feeding – *if that's what it was* – off the girl? Perhaps weeks, maybe longer. How much longer? If this place was as she suspected caught in a time warp, some kind of Groundhog Day, he could have been feeding off her for *years.* The thought of it made Lizzie's heart race – although it hadn't stopped pounding ever since she'd seen him earlier.

What could she do against him if he was a demon? The Pisaca was almost invulnerable, guns had been useless against her. The only thing that had stopped her was the holy Lingam of Shiva, which she'd wanted for some reason but which had, when she grabbed it with her bare hands, finally blasted her to who knows where. Lizzie shuddered, remembering that awful standoff on the moonlit Kashi ghat, the Pisaca negotiating with her friends whilst keeping a sharp talon on Lizzie's throat.

Maybe the Lingam could kill Mr Paterson? *A lot of help, even if it could.*

She didn't know what she was going to do. *Besides keep her wits about her.*

Maybe he wasn't a demon, anyway – just some hillbilly freak who fancied himself as some kind of vampire. *What a comforting thought.* Suddenly she felt the truck brake sharply and judder to a halt.

'Come on Hector, let's take this one down.'

Hector? *Was there someone else in the cab?*

Unmistakably, she heard the sound of *both* doors opening, and two people climbing out. Their footsteps crunched on the gravel road and then swished away through the grass. She held her breath, lifted the tarpaulin, and peeped out over the edge of the tailgate.

Mr Paterson was standing just down off the road near a tree stump. There was a young Afro-Caribbean boy with him, dressed in a navy shirt and knee-length shorts. The boy had a long, scrawny afro.

Obviously that was Hector. Lizzie suspected from the boy's posture, the way his arms hung at his sides, that he was a plat eye.

'Come on now, boy, just pull it down,' said Mr Paterson. The boy stepped forward and took hold of the top of the tree stump. He didn't look particularly strong, but Lizzie saw the intensity of his expression as he tried to pull the boggy stump over.

And then she noticed something on the bark-less stump – a few scratches, no, thin *lines* – and realised that it was one of the symbols she had seen on her tour of the bayou.

Had the symbols been done by Mr Paterson? If so, why? And why was he taking them down now?

Whilst the boy was clearly putting his heart and soul into pushing over the stump, it soon became clear he wasn't going to succeed. Lizzie winced as Mr Paterson suddenly struck him across the top of the head.

'Stand back,' he said, and the boy stumbled back a couple of steps. Mr Paterson drew a large knife from his belt and began to hack repeatedly at the symbol. Soon it was a twisted mess of splintered wood.

'Now go get the chain,' he said, standing up straight and producing a handkerchief, with which he proceeded to mop his brow.

Lizzie ducked back under the canvas as Hector turned and headed back toward the truck. Again she held her breath as there were a couple of metallic clunks at the front of the vehicle, followed by a sea-on-shingle sound that was surely the unwinding of a long chain.

She waited in the half-darkness as the pair of them worked on wrapping the chain around the tree stump. They then came back to the cab and Mr Paterson started the engine. The tyres skidded and kicked up gravel, then bit, and the vehicle began to reverse.

And then something strange happened. Bent up under the tarpaulin, Lizzie felt a jumbled series of jerks and spasms inside her and all around, accompanied by images of striking ravens, singing children, and daylight *imprinted* with darkness, suns flashing on moons, dirty, muddy rains falling across shining blue skies.

As soon as the strange, staccato experience started it was over.

The truck stopped and Mr Paterson turned off the engine. Lizzie twisted her fingers through her hair, trying to re-orientate herself, to shake the weirdness from her mind. She hadn't heard the stump come up, but guessed they must have been successful because this time only one of the cabin doors opened. Someone went out and unfastened the chain from the stump, then returned to the vehicle. Lizzie heard them winding the chain back slowly on the winch.

'That's it, just takes the one to go down,' said Mr Paterson, stepping back up into the cab. 'Welcome to the twenty-first century, Hector!'

Lizzie put her hand up to her mouth as the truck coughed back to life, and drew away.

*

It wasn't long after the incident at the tree trunk that the truck stopped again.

Lizzie began to panic, her mind racing. What if Mr Paterson opened the dropside? What would she do? *What was he going to do if he found her?*

The doors opened and she heard them both climb out. She was breathing fast, but concentrated hard to catch her breath. She was petrified.

After a few moments she breathed out. They must have gone away somewhere. She waited a little longer, wishing her heart would stop its furious pounding. Then, when she realised it was never going to, she lifted the edge of the tarpaulin and once again peeped over the side of the truck.

Her jaw dropped at the sight before her.

The vehicle had pulled up at the edge of the road. There was a clearing amongst a fringe of trees lining the calm brown waters of the lagoon. Within the clearing was a single gnarled old tree, whose branches stretched out dark and low across the rank-smelling water. Mr

Paterson and the boy Hector were standing in front of the tree.

And they were surrounded by plat eyes.

Lizzie's hand clamped over her mouth, a moment too late to stop her gasp. Thankfully there seemed enough movement and activity around the ancient tree for no one to notice her.

She recognised several of the plat eyes now. There was the bearded white man, who had caught hold of her out on the bayou and whom she had cut with the knife, the black teenage boy she'd seen on her first night near Cypress House, another man who had lumbered after her as she followed the force-field – and there, near to the water's edge, was Miles Day himself, in his fine but frayed mauve jacket, with his spectacles still in place.

Mr Paterson was walking among the plat eyes, feeding each one of them with something from a small bowl. They were standing there, dropping their jaws open as he came along with the strange, greyish paste, and rubbed it on their tongues and lips. It was a bizarre process, like a parade inspection. Once he'd smeared the final remnants of the bowl in Hector's mouth, he turned and began to address the plat eyes before him, like a Captain talking to his troops.

'You, Hank, and you, Devlin, I want you to go back to the farm and bring a couple of chickens in a cage, keep 'em here for later. Make one of them a very fine red rooster. Plus I'll need the knife and cups, the

134

candles and all the other ceremonial stuff. Gotta make it look good, don't we!

'Miles and Tony, you go up to the road and check that no one comes down now the runes are down. That ole' *Road Closed* sign's done its job, no one's been down here in fifty-three years, but we don't want to be taking any risks now. If any one does come, kill them at the fallen tree.

'Jake, John, Winnie – I want you all back at the house, keepin' watch again. They haven't come out in all this time, but now things have changed and they might sense it in their bones. Not that there's far they can go, what with madam in her chair and that ole witch as out of shape as a bent politician's grin.

'Now Drake, I want you to go meet our guest later. Bring her to join us at the house after dark.

'Mike, Hector, you come with me in the truck. We're gonna go check all the runes have gone down OK. Hoodoo this strong can take a while to finish for good, and we don't want anything strange happening now.

'Everyone else, duties as normal.'

Mr Paterson turned around slowly, as if appraising his men. He sniffed in deeply.

'Oh – and anyone find any snakes, bring 'em back. And we all meet back here for showdown.' He smiled, then chuckled. 'They say they needed a cupful of witchkin blood to revive Her Glorious Ladyship through the phylactery. Well, they already got that, and now we're gonna give 'em a whole gallon more of the stuff after this Conjure of Sacrifice. Which'll have the added benefit of getting me all the remaining years of the girl's life, if their big plan don't come off!'

'Uhh!'

Lizzie glanced right and froze as she saw one of the plat eyes, a bald middle-aged man, standing at the edge of the group and pointing at her. All eyes, sharp and milky, turned toward her.

'Arr – Urrn – Haar...' rose the cries, as the creatures began to lumber towards the truck.

Without thinking, Lizzie stood up and leapt out over the dropside. She landed awkwardly, and felt her knee jar as she tried to upright herself. Then she was flat on her side in the dust, having lost her balance. She stared in horror over her shoulder as the plat eyes advanced quickly on her, the bald man in dungarees first, arms outstretched.

She screamed and pushed herself up. Then she was running – with a slight hobble – as fast as she could away, back up the dirt road, away. Soon she had turned a bend and disappeared into the woods.

'Stop!' yelled Mr Paterson, and the plat eyes, strewn up the road, stopped.

'The-the-there all along,' Hector said.

'I know,' he said. 'I don't know what she's up to, but there's one thing I do know. Ain't nothing to fear from a little girl.'

Chapter 13: The Fight in the Cellar

By the time Raj and Pandu came to the kitchen, the final room on the ground floor, it was almost dark, and increasingly difficult to make things out.

'Shall I turn on the light, Uncle?' said Pandu.

'No, don't risk it,' said Raj. 'Look at all those halogens in the ceiling – that house across the road, or anyone visiting the church would be able to see us. Let's just be quick and get out of here – it looks like the place has been empty for weeks, or even months.'

'Or not...' said Pandu, standing near the toaster and holding up an open loaf of bread.

'Yes – and look here,' said Raj, staring into the lit fridge. Looking inside, Pandu saw that whilst it was largely empty there were a few basic items – milk, butter, jam.

The Inspector opened the milk and sniffed it. 'Fresh,' he said.

'Maybe the housekeeper?' said Pandu.

'Maybe.'

On one of the interior walls Pandu found two small pine doors. The first opened to reveal a larder, with shelves emptied except for some tinned items. A few onions on the floor had gone mouldy and given the room a musty, unpleasant smell.

The second door opened to reveal a flight of stone steps running down, presumably into the cellar.

'Uncle – look!' whispered Pandu and Raj set down a photo of a woman on a horse that he'd been holding up to the window to see, and hurried over.

A bare light bulb poked out from a socket on the wall below – and it was on.

After exchanging a look, Raj drew out his Glock revolver and began to descend the steps. Pandu followed.

At the bottom of the stairs was a damp, narrow corridor, again lit by a couple of bare bulbs. There were two shut doors on the right hand side and one on the left. At the far end of the corridor was another door, half open with light spilling out of it. As the two companions stopped and listened they could hear voices coming from the room beyond. A man and a woman were talking to each other, but their voices were too muffled to make out anything they were saying.

'We have to get closer,' Raj whispered into Pandu's ear.

Pandu nodded and they began to creep as quietly as they could down the passage.

When they were about halfway down they could hear what the woman was saying:

'...we know Paterson's a fool, but he's a dangerous fool. He's clearly the offspring of an Arch Witch, no one else would be able to make such a time hex, even with the power of a tirtha to draw on.'

'It's her!' Pandu whispered heatedly to Raj, who nodded sharply.

'Lucky he had such a crush on the Mistress,' said the man, who sounded Chinese. 'And that she was able to persuade him to give her the Book.'

'I don't trust him,' said Lamya. 'He claims he understands what we need Caroline for, but I still think he's going to kill her for this *Conjure of Sacrifice*. He'd rather use her to extend his own life than save her for the Final Sacrifice.'

'I agree,' said the Chinese man. 'He's unreliable. But how are we going to stop him without jeopardising the girl or her Artefact, that shaman's doll?'

'What I want to know is how he ever found out about the tirtha and Book in the first place?' interrupted a third voice, much more refined and entitled, *English*, than the other two.

'By chance, apparently,' said the Chinese man. 'Paterson told the full story to the Mistress. He was an orderly doing national service in the Pacific when he befriended Caroline's other brother Henry. Henry was badly injured in some training drill. He caught a fever and let slip about The Book of Life and the tirtha when he was delirious. After that Paterson smothered him – or so he claimed.'

'Do you know who they're talking about?' whispered Raj to Pandu.

'No,' said Pandu.

'...after he'd finished in the Marines he tracked Miles and Caroline down to Cypress House, ingratiated himself, and convinced Miles to let him take on odd jobs,' continued the Chinese man. 'At the same time he started using Hoodoo to create the plat eyes, to frighten off the locals and search – unsuccessfully – for the tirtha. In the end he used his time hex to fix on a single day in September 1961, so he could extend his life indefinitely by feeding off Caroline's witchkin blood, and keep others away from the Book. Not that he knew anyone who could translate it, fortunately.

'But whilst no one except him could pass through the hex's boundary, the portal in the Garden gave us – and the Mistress – a way in...'

There was a strange sound, something high, like a hiss. Pandu made the connection between the noise and its producer at the same moment as that producer – a dog, sniffing – poked its snout around the open door.

At once the dog – a brown and white spaniel – began to bark fiercely, and scamper down the corridor towards them.

'Run!' hissed Raj, but before they even turned they noticed that something extraordinary was happening – the dog was growing as it charged towards them, its legs stretching and its body bulking out. Worse still, its face was transforming into something far uglier and fiercer, with curved fangs and ferocious, obsidian eyes.

'Shiva's arms!' shouted Raj. He began to fire off rounds at the creature as it hurtled forward.

The first bullet hit the ground behind the dog but the second and third struck home, sending the hellish creature flying back into the wall with an astonished yelp. At the same moment, another overgrown, demonic-looking spaniel appeared at the doorway, followed closely by a bald, young Chinese man. Pandu also caught a glimpse of Lamya, in her western clothes, behind him and, for the briefest second, a grey-haired man – before Raj was thrusting him back towards the stairs.

'Get out!' cried the Inspector.

'Get them!' shouted the bald man. The second dog pounded down the passage towards them, followed quickly by the fast-recuperating first.

'No, no, no...' muttered Raj as he continued shooting, all the time backing up. Pandu was at the stairs first and was just about to start jumping up them when the second dog, bleeding profusely from the jaw and flank, sprang up and sunk its teeth into the Inspector's gun arm. Raj cried out in pain, and two more bullets struck the ground. The dog thrashed its head about violently, causing the Inspector's fingers to loosen and the gun to clatter on the ground. In the next moment the second dog launched itself at the policeman and struck him full force in the chest. Raj fell back and hit the ground.

Pandu jumped forward, hoping to get to the gun, but the two giant dogs on top of the struggling Inspector now blocked the narrow corridor. A quick glance back down the passage showed him that the

Chinese man and Lamya were bearing down on them too.

He looked down at Raj and saw the look of furious intent in the Inspector's eyes as he used all his remaining strength to keep the jaws of the first dog away from his face and neck. The second dog continued savaging the Inspector's limp gun arm. With no weapons to hand, Pandu reached out and grabbed the first by its ears, but it ignored him and continued to thrust and bite at the Inspector's face and neck. Pandu pulled as hard as he could and felt one of the ears rip in his hand.

'Get out!' shouted Raj.

Pandu looked down and saw the pleading, the terror, in his friend's eyes.

'Get out – while – you – can!'

Pandu realised the hopelessness of the situation, the desperation of his friend's plea.

With tears blurring his vision, he turned and sprang away up the steps.

*

'Delly – Star – after him!' shouted the Chinese man.

'Quick!' Lamya added.

Raj felt the awful pressure of the dogs' jaws release, and then their terrible weight was off him. He wanted – wanted with all his will, *help me Lord Shiva, help me now* – to sit upright and retrieve his revolver. But his body wouldn't obey him, and whilst he could still see and hear – albeit with some fogginess – he knew his injuries

142

must be severe, and that it was only the adrenalin keeping him from losing consciousness – or worse.

He just hoped Pandu had got away.

He looked up then and it was her he saw, the chrysalis of evil, the Kali priestess, Lamya, advancing quickly towards him.

'Time we finished you off for good, Inspector,' she said.

He saw her arm rise, the curved blade in her hand.

Chapter 14: A Hard Rain

With the first few drops of rain, Lizzie knew things had changed.

By the time the gothic roof of Cypress House came into sight the skies had opened and water was pounding the dry road with relish. She was soaked through and hobbling on her aching knee when she reached the porch and climbed the steps up to the front door.

She banged hard with her fist, wondering if she would be greeted by a wizened old black woman and a blonde sixty-something year old.

When there was no answer she banged again, and then shouted: 'Let me in! Let me in! There's a crowd of plat eyes coming this way, and Mr Paterson is a demon!'

Just when she remembered that the back door would probably be open and turned away she heard bolts being drawn behind her. Moments later the door swung open.

'Get inside!' Lola hissed. She looked exactly the same as she did when Lizzie left her. *Obviously the time catch-up hadn't suddenly aged the house's occupants.*

Lizzie went in, clasping her wet knee.

'Every time...' Lola began.

Lizzie marched straight past her, down the corridor and into the living room. Lola followed.

'Stop! Stop right there, child...'

Caroline was in her usual position near the fireplace, cradling Sally Ally and reading an old book. She looked up as Lizzie came in.

'Where have you been?' she said.

'I've been out of the house, risking my life to find out what's really going on in this psychoville.'

'You're wet.'

'Yes. Have you noticed how it's raining?'

'I'll give her a bath an' get her changed...'

'No!' Lizzie said, turning and holding the flat of her hand out to stop the woman.

'You...'

'Look. I'm going to tell you how it is. Or at least how it is in as much as I've worked out so far. You'd better listen carefully because we're in extreme danger. And we need to get out of here fast.'

Caroline and Lola looked at her, an almost identical mix of anger and confusion on their faces.

'Those things out there, the plat eyes, are not being kept out by Lola's spells. They're being kept out by orders, the orders of the man who made them. Mr Paterson. It's him, not *Ole Man Hoodoo* or any other fancy man who's behind all this. It's him who's created those plat eyes – by giving those poor men some kind of paste or potion – and he's made them to keep you in.'

'What? You're speakin' nonsense, girl. It's my wards that's keeping 'em out.'

'No it's not. I'm sure of it now. There are people who can do magical things. But you're not one of them.'

Lola started to protest again but Lizzie carried on.

'You've both been trapped in this place for longer than you think, a lot longer. I don't know how long exactly, but he – Mr Paterson – has created some special... *runes*... and used magic, really powerful magic, to somehow make time repeat itself around here. I don't know how he's done it, but he's trapped you in time, I think. And the rest of the world has moved on.'

'What in hell's name are you talking about?' said Caroline.

'What year is it?' said Lizzie.

'Silly question,' said Caroline, glancing at Lola.

'Come on – tell me.'

'It's 1961,' said Lola.

'And what date?'

'Why... now...' Lola began.

'September!' said Caroline.

'Yes, that's it, September,' said Lola.

Lizzie paused, staring at Caroline. 'You know. You *know*. Deep down, things aren't right. They haven't been working properly. You've been caught in a trap. That's why, how, you managed to get that message to me on my first night, out on the swamp.'

Caroline's expression remained sceptical.

'Look, there's something really special about you, Caroline,' said Lizzie, throwing a slightly apologetic glance at Lola. 'I think you have some sort of power, I don't know what exactly, but it's at the heart of all this. It's why Mr Paterson trapped you in here all those years ago, it's why he visits you every day and... and takes some of your blood. He needs it for something, and my guess is that it's to keep him alive, or at least to prolong his life. I knew someone – some*thing* – once who was like that too....'

'Oh, now hold on. Blood? What are you talkin' about now?' interjected Lola. 'He's just giving her some medicine, for the haemophilia.'

'No, he's not. I don't think Caroline has haemophilia at all. She's got the symptoms, all right. But that's because he's syringing half a pint of blood out of her arm every day.'

'What?' said Caroline.

'Yes – and there's something important about that doll, too. He did something... *strange* with it. Held it up to his face and cuddled it, after you'd passed out. I think it might have something to do with his plan too.'

'Sally Ally?' said Caroline, looking incredulously at the wooden figure.

'It's not a doll, really, is it? It's more like a small primitive statue, of a shaman or something,' said Lizzie.

'Look, he's got you both under some kind of spell,' she continued. 'So you don't realise – or fully realise – what he's doing. But you both know it, don't you? You know I'm right, he's up to no good.'

'Never heard so much rubbish in my life,' said Lola. 'It's time you stopped makin' up stories...'

Lizzie looked at her. 'I am having to make some of it up, based on what I've seen and heard. And on what I've experienced before... in my own life. But I'm sure most of it is true. I got in his truck just now and watched him and a plat eye kid pulling down runes, talking about time returning to normal, getting the rest of the plat eyes together down by the lake. He's planning some kind of major showdown later today. Something terrible, he was talking about blood. That's why we need to get out.

'How long is it since you remember it raining in the afternoon? How long is it since you remember eating properly instead of just picking at your food? You know it in your bones, I know it sounds incredible, but I think you've been here for *years*...'

Lola emitted a harsh laugh – but Lizzie could see Caroline's expression softening towards her. *She knew, she had to know.*

Lizzie's mind was racing so fast, she was starting to feel dizzy. A painful silence had descended on them all. Then she remembered the one big question she'd never asked, and said:

'There is one thing I need to know. How come neither of you have ever asked who I am or where I came from?'

'Because we know,' said Caroline.

148

Chapter 15: Preparing for Siege

The dogs bounded through the garden gate and Pandu held his breath, perched precariously on the wall above.

He watched their dark shadows – now shrunk back to normal size – as they charged off through the churchyard towards the kissing gate, following his scent towards the village.

How long did he have? They might go all the way back to Rowan Cottage or, if they were super-intelligent, they might realise that a boy would never be able to run that fast and come back to check whether they had made a mistake.

Which of course they had, as he'd used the frames for the climbing shrubs to hastily clamber up to the top of the old wall.

But what was he going to do now?

His mind was a storm of confusion and abject, awful grief. He was sure Raj was dead. There was no way *she* would have spared him.

What should he do?

His first instinct was to go back into the house to avenge his friend. He could get a knife, one of those big kitchen knives, and go back and fight the priestess and the men to the death. He would lose, he knew, he was no innate killer like them – but at least he might have the satisfaction of wounding one of them. *Which, right now, he so much wanted to do, more than anything ever.*

But just as he was about to climb down and do it, go back in, his reason got the better of him. What about Lizzie? And Ashlyn? He needed to let them know what was going on in the hellish basement of this house, right in the heart of the village. Something major and utterly evil was being hatched, he was sure of it. And if he went and died a vengeful but futile death in the cellar, the knowledge of that evil would die with him.

He thought of his friend, the terror and pleading in his eyes at the end.

He owed it to the Inspector to do the thing that was right, not the thing he wanted most to do. Otherwise Raj would have died in vain.

He pinched the bridge of his nose, and tears flooded over his hands. Two loud sobs wrenched themselves from his throat, he was unable to contain them.

He had to think quick.

Ashlyn's house was closer to the village than Lizzie's, he knew – but he didn't know where it was exactly. So, like a world-class acrobat, he ran fifty yards in the opposite direction to the dogs along the wall, then found an adjacent garden alongside the churchyard that he was able to climb down into. Thankfully all the lights of this house were off, and he made his way down its side passage and back out on to the street.

He had to duck back quickly behind the front wall of the house, hearing the footsteps of someone emerge from the lane to the church. *Was it one of them from the basement?* He couldn't know, but dared not check in case he stumbled back into the dogs. He guessed it was more likely to be someone from one of the other houses down the lane, even though it was getting late now.

The village layout was relatively simple, it was easy to take a couple of back streets that let him keep well away from the noses of the monster dogs. Soon he was out of the village and heading back through the fields towards Lizzie's house. He prayed that the dogs had realised he couldn't have got so far and had returned to try and find his scent back at the house.

All the while that he ran, he was choking back tears.

*

'You *knew* I was coming?'

Caroline gave a small nod. Lola continued to stare at Lizzie.

'How?'

Caroline and Lola looked at each other, then Caroline looked back at Lizzie and said:

'My Aunt – Aunty Evelyn – visited us a long time ago, when my father was away. She appeared out of nowhere one day in a fine long skirt but soaked to the skin, just like you. After getting dry she stayed for a whole afternoon and had tea with us on the verandah. She told us lots of things, like how she didn't see eye to eye with my father over the war, and how he had taken an important book from their home in England, which she could never forgive him for.'

'Where was your father?'

'Away on a reading tour. He was becoming quite renowned as a poet at the time.'

'New York,' said Lola. 'He was in New York.'

'That's when she gave me Sally Ally, she said she was a special, blessed doll and that she would look after me if I looked after her. So I have, all these years. And she is special.'

'So your Aunty Evelyn came visiting,' said Lizzie. 'But you still haven't told me how you knew I was coming.'

'She told us. She said that some time in the future we would be in trouble, but that we didn't need to worry because my English cousin would come and help us. And here you are. Everything was so strange when you first arrived, and it took us a while to remember properly what she'd said to us. To be honest, we hadn't taken her very seriously at the time, she seemed kind of... *eccentric*. Nice, but eccentric. And then, when we remembered, we had to be sure you were the girl she meant, not just some other perverse corruption of the swamp, like the plat eyes.'

Lizzie felt her skin shrinking with goose pimples. How on earth did Evelyn know that she was coming? *She died years before Lizzie was born.* She cupped her head in her hands.

'This is all so weird,' she muttered.

Then she thought of something else Caroline had said. 'What was the book?' she asked.

'She didn't say much about it,' said Caroline. 'But she didn't have to. We already knew what she was talking about, and where it was. My father kept it in his bureau under lock and key, and he'd expressly forbidden us to go in there. But the day after she left I searched for the key – my disease hadn't set in then – and found it.'

'What was it like?' said Lizzie.

'Big and old. *Very old.* Made of leather, with brown silky pages almost falling apart. It was very beautiful, written in lovely black ink, I think it was Chinese or Japanese. There were lots of drawings, line drawings, in it, mainly landscapes but also abstract diagrams and several pictures of mythical-looking creatures, oriental dragons and lions and such. But I don't remember much else about it.'

Lizzie looked at Lola, who momentarily avoided her gaze.

'It's not in the bureau now, is it?' Lizzie said, continuing to stare at the woman.

'Why not?' said Caroline.

'I broke into it yesterday,' said Lizzie. 'It was empty.'

Caroline looked at Lola. 'Where's it gone?' she said.

'I don't know,' said Lola, shrugging defensively. 'I wouldn't be surprised if she's taken it and keepin' it a secret.'

'I haven't!' said Lizzie.

'Be quiet, girl!' said Lola. 'It's time you went an' laid down in your room.'

'No, we need to get out…'

'Thinkin' you're gonna solve things…'

'Who else is going to solve things?' shrieked Lizzie.

'Mr Miles, when he gets…'

'Miles is a plat eye.'

'What?' said Caroline.

'He's one of them,' said Lizzie quietly. Then she added, looking down at the carpet: 'I found his car last night when I was out on the swamp, following the perimeter of the force field that's trapping us in here. The car was crushed under a fallen tree. Miles was in it.'

'That can't be…' said Caroline, a look of horror on her face.

'It is, I'm sure. He was wearing a purple jacket, wasn't he? And he's got long wavy hair, and he's very handsome. Wears glasses.'

'There's a picture by your bed,' said Lola.

'Yes. That's how I recognised him.'

'He can't be one of them! Not Miles…' said Caroline, tears welling in her eyes.

'I'm sorry,' said Lizzie.

'No, you're not sorry,' said Lola. 'You're makin' things up! Mr Miles is not a plat eye!'

'He is!'

'He…quick!' Lola exclaimed, dashing over to Caroline. Lizzie looked round at the girl and saw that her eyes had rolled upwards and she was shaking in her chair. She ran over to her.

'What can I do?' she said.

'Let's take her down to her room,' said Lola. 'She needs rest.'

'But we can't put her to bed – we have to get out,' said Lizzie. 'The plat eyes are coming!'

'Maybe you should have thought of that before you went and told her her beloved brother was dead…'

Lizzie glanced worriedly at the window.

*

Once they had moved Caroline down the hall and lifted her out of her chair and into bed she began to return to consciousness.

'Would you like a drink, child?' said Lola.

'Yes, please.' Lola went off to the kitchen.

Lizzie sat on a small padded stool by the bed. She noticed clean handkerchiefs in an open bedside drawer. She took one out and dabbed the girl's damp brow.

'How often do you have these fits?' said Lizzie.

'Not often. Only during a crisis.'

'Do you think you might have had a small one on the night I arrived on the swamp?'

'Maybe.'

'You saved my life,' said Lizzie. 'I'm sure I would have died if I'd got lost out there with the plat eyes. Do you remember anything about coming to me that night?'

Caroline stared ahead, her gaze focused somewhere beyond Lizzie's shoulder.

'When you say that happened I can't… disbelieve you. No, I don't remember anything. But what you say

155

feels like it might just be true. I think I was having a dream, but I only remember little flitting bits, more the feel of it than anything distinct. There was a sense of urgency, the dark bayou and the plat eyes – although they're always in my dreams – but I do, vaguely, recall another person there. Someone that seemed in need, and important. But that's all...'

'Back where I come from there are these witches – well, Wiccans, I should say – who I used to think were a bunch of weirdoes but it turned out they were OK, and some of them really do have strange... *abilities*. My great-uncle was one of them – and I think you might have inherited some of those abilities too.'

Lizzie was surprised – and relieved – to see Caroline laugh.

'You saying I'm a witch?'

'No! Not like that...'

They were laughing together when Lola came back in with fresh milk in a glass.

'There you are, Miss Caroline,' she said, passing it to the girl.

Caroline began to quaff it greedily, watched by an amazed Lizzie. Soon the glass was empty.

'I'm feeling hungry, too,' said Caroline.

'Now you mention it, my tummy's grumbling like a volcano,' said Lola. 'Shall I go cook us some dinner?'

The urgency of their situation sprang back into Lizzie's mind. 'No – we have to get out of here!' she said, dashing over to one of the windows and opening the shutters wide.

'Oh God, they're here already!' she said.

There were two plat eyes standing at the bottom of the lawn in the pouring rain, staring at her through the window. They looked ghastly – ghastly and bedraggled. She closed the shutters.

'Is the back door locked?' she said to Lola.

'Um – I don't know...'

Without another word, Lizzie ran through to the kitchen. There were more plat eyes in the back yard around the tree, including the middle aged bald one who had spotted her in the truck and the one she'd had a fight with on the swamp. The rain was so heavy now it was blasting up small bits of grit and stone from the ground.

She turned the key in the door to lock it and closed its two bolts. Then she went round every room on the ground floor, checking for plat eyes – there were *plenty* – and closing and fastening all the shutters.

What were they going to do?

She could see they were trapped in now. Whilst she was fairly sure the time magic was broken so they could in theory get to other places and ask *real people* for help, there was no way she could think of to get Caroline out past the plat eyes. *How could they flee down a pot-holed road pushing a girl in a wheelchair?*

She tried to remember what Mr Paterson had been saying to his assembly of plat eyes. He had talked about a witch, she thought, about needing some blood for something. Wasn't that bound to be Caroline's blood, as he was already using it for his obscure, nasty purposes? It was easy to make the connection, now she was alone and thinking straight. But then she remembered the chilling words he'd said just before the bald plat eye had spotted her and everything had gone crazy. Something about giving them *a gallon of the stuff. Surely... no... surely he wasn't planning to kill her?*

She ran down the hall and burst into Caroline's room. The blonde girl had been lying in her bed dozing whilst Lola prepared the food, but her eyes opened wide with the noise of the door swinging open and banging against the wall.

'We have to get you upstairs!' said Lizzie. 'Now!'

'What? I can't...'

'I'll get Lola and we'll help you up,' said Lizzie.

'But why...?'

'The plat eyes have surrounded us.'

'They're *always* there!'

'There's more of them now, all round the building. I think Mr Paterson is... I think he's planning something.'

'Planning what?'

'Something bad. Trust me. We need to get upstairs. Is there an attic in this place?'

*

Lizzie looked up at the dark rectangle in the roof, and the wooden ladder that rose up to it.

No way. No way were they going to get *Miss Day* up there.

So what were they going to do?

They were going to have to shut themselves in one of the rooms. All of them had locks, so one was just as good as another, she reasoned. *May as well go for the one she knew, her room.*

When she got back downstairs both Lola and Caroline were in the girl's bedroom, wolfing down thick sandwiches filled with meat, cheese, tomato and relish. Caroline was propped up against the pillows, whilst Lola was straddling the bedside stool.

'Come on,' said Lizzie. 'We have to get upstairs, it's safer.'

'Let's just finish these,' said Lola, her mouth full.

'Finish them upstairs!'

She could see the indifference on their faces. They clearly weren't as worried about the plat eyes as her.

'Remember what Evelyn said to you,' said Lizzie. 'I'm your *saviour*. Now come on, let's get you out of bed and upstairs!'

Lola reluctantly put her half-eaten sandwich back on her plate and set it down on the bedside table. They lifted Caroline out and into her wheelchair, while the girl continued to cram sandwich into her mouth.

'Jeez!' said Lizzie, although she was starting to feel so ravenous she was considering taking a bite out of the girl's sandwich without even asking.

Outside, there was a distant rumble of thunder.

'Is it the Big One?' said Lola. 'Is Carla finally here?'

'No, I don't think so,' said Lizzie, as they struggled with Caroline's weight. 'Just a spring storm.'

'Spring?'

'I'll explain later.'

They wheeled Caroline down the hall to the base of the staircase.

'I think I can manage a few steps,' said Caroline as they lifted her out, supporting her around the shoulders. Slowly, they all made their way up the stairs and then down the landing into Charles Day's old bedroom, the Bird Room. Lola was panting as they lowered Caroline into the armchair.

'Are you all right?' said Lizzie, and the woman nodded.

'Just a little out of shape,' she muttered, easing upright and clutching her lower back.

Lizzie crossed to the window and looked out. She counted seven plat eyes in the increasing gloom, standing around like ghoulish monuments in the driving rain. Lola came up and stood by her, looking out too.

At the same moment their eyes alighted on the most distant plat eye with wavy hair plastered against his scalp, a purple jacket, and horn-rimmed glasses worn at a slightly odd angle. Lizzie and Lola exchanged a meaningful glance, then stepped back. Lizzie pushed the shutters to.

'Our friends are still out there, I presume?' said Caroline.

'We need to be able to defend ourselves,' said Lizzie. 'Are there any guns in the house?'

'Guns?' said Lola.

'You planning to shoot someone?' said Caroline.

'Not planning to,' said Lizzie. 'But it might be better to have one, just as a bluff.'

'You ever use a gun?' said Lola.

'Can't be that hard,' said Lizzie.

Lola laughed.

'Why are we even talking about this?' said Caroline. 'No, there are no guns in the house.'

'I thought every house in America had a gun,' said Lizzie.

'Well you're wrong.'

'What else can we use?' said Lizzie. 'Come on, think!'

'How do we even know they're planning to come in?' said Lola.

'I'm still starving,' said Caroline.

'OK, OK, stop!' said Lizzie. 'Lola, you come downstairs with me and get some more food. I'll think about what we do to defend ourselves.'

*

Whilst Lola was preparing more food – *frying onions and bacon, Jeez, that smelled so good, but didn't she realise the danger they were in?* – Lizzie ran, or rather *hobbled* around on her achy knee, doing all she could to make Cypress House more impregnable.

She jammed a chair hard up under the handle of the front door and got Lola to divert briefly from her fry up to help her move the heavy kitchen table up against the back door. She stacked a load of hefty-but-still-chuckable items at the top of the stairs, including an antique chair, the china birds from her room, and a beautiful lamp hand-painted with flowers. Then she partially blocked the bottom of the stairs with the telephone table, another chair, a sturdy coat stand and

161

an umbrella holder. At the last minute she pulled out all the old umbrellas and opened them up, cluttering up the hall area between the door and the stairs. She left enough room for herself and Lola to go back up, intending to block it as they went.

Then she went into the kitchen and found the knife block. She examined all those yellow handles.

And realised she couldn't take one. She'd hated cutting that man's hand, and wasn't going to do it again. She could smash things over people's heads, fight by pushing and thumping – but she didn't want to stab anyone, it was just way too nasty. *And so much more likely to kill.*

In the end she picked up a rolling pin, and helped Lola carry all the delicious-smelling plates of fried food and bread back up to the Bird Room.

*

It was very late when Pandu finally reached the gravel lane that led up to Rowan Cottage.

He had lost time in the fields when he'd had to hide behind a hedge from a group of high-spirited young men coming loudly down a footpath which intersected with his. He guessed that they had been returning from that world-renowned British tradition of going to the pub. Then, with the lack of any moonlight to navigate by he'd managed to get completely lost for what felt like hours. Finally he'd stumbled out on to a road which he'd guessed – correctly, it turned out – was the one that led to Rowan Cottage. Now, standing in front of the cottage sign, he dug out his mobile to check the time. 5.42 am. Which was Indian time, of course, so here it must be... 1.12 am, four and a half hours earlier. *Lizzie must be in bed.*

As he crept down the drive he wondered what he was going to say to her. How would she react to his news, the news of Raj's death? What should they do? He thought the most sensible thing would be for them to go to Ashlyn's. They needed an adult to help them now.

And what about Lizzie's mum? He knew that Lizzie had kept *everything* about the tirthas secret from her, she didn't know anything about the surreal second life her daughter led. She didn't know about Eva, the Lingam, or the Kashi murders. Lizzie had always said she thought it would drive her mum crazy, she wouldn't be able to cope and would move her away immediately. And she would probably tell the police or press. *What would happen then?*

But as he reached the quiet, unlit house Pandu started to wonder if it might actually be time for the world to know about the tirthas. If there was something evil going on, shouldn't all the world's forces for good be marshalled against it?

It was doing his head in, just thinking about it. One thing was for sure, it wasn't a decision he would make on his own. He would get Lizzie and Ashlyn, and the other witches in the village if necessary, to discuss it. It would be a joint decision, whatever they decided to do.

He stood before the front door and thought. *If he rang the doorbell that was it – mother involved, no real options.*

And how would he explain himself, the anxious, crazy way he undoubtedly looked? She would probably think he was a down-and-out and call the police straight away.

No, he had to see if he could get to Lizzie alone.

He diverted down the side passage, along past the kitchen window.

Chapter 16: The Figures in the Storm

Lizzie had just tucked into her bacon sandwich when there was a loud crash downstairs.

She put her plate down and ran over to the window, followed by Lola. She fumbled with the shutter catch. Thunder boomed as she finally swung back the shutters.

In the darkness, she could hear the rain hammering the ground, beating down on the slide, paddling pool and other children's bric-a-brac that was scattered about the overgrown lawn.

'Turn off the light!' she said.

Caroline reached over and switched off the bedside lamp.

With the light out, Lizzie's eyes acclimatised swiftly to the dark. She could see the plat eyes, darker forms on the grey-black grass, advancing towards the house. One was in the process of mounting the steps to the porch. *With all that noise coming from downstairs, there had to be another already on the porch, smashing one of the windows.*

She strained her eyes to see further back into the darkness, to the area at the edge of the swamp beneath the encroaching trees. She spotted two more figures, one tall and the other much shorter. The top of the tall one's head was grey, which she figured was probably a hat or – *more likely* – the white cap of Mr Paterson. She shuddered, wondering if that was Hector beside him, although whoever it was did seem taller than Hector. Maybe the boy plat eye was standing on a stump or something?

There was more banging from downstairs, almost certainly the shutters of the broken window being thumped.

'What are we going to do?' said Caroline.

'Don't worry, no one can get past my wards,' said Lola.

Once again Lizzie wasn't so sure. After all, the back door had been open for Mr Paterson. *She was sure the plat eyes could have come in whenever they – or their master – wanted.*

The downstairs shutters banged again.

'I'm going to go and see what's happening,' said Lizzie, still staring out of the window. *Was it Hector?* 'You stay here and look after Caroline.'

'OK.'

As Lizzie was about to turn away from the window a flash of lightning lit up the stretch of ground near the swamp. She froze as she saw the two figures fully, if momentarily, illuminated.

Yes, the tall man with the cap was of course Mr Paterson.

But the figure beside him wasn't Hector. It was a woman, a woman whose short-cropped, soaking black hair framed a very distinctive, round face. *A woman Lizzie had seen only once before, but whom she remembered well because she knew so much about her.*

Lizzie's heart thumped wildly as she stared in disbelief at the Kali priestess, Lamya.

What was *she* doing here?

Staring through the darkness at the faint outlines of the man and woman, Lizzie's brain whirled in panic and incomprehension.

Lamya had been caught after a fight with Pandu and the police at Manikarnika ghat, and as far as Lizzie knew she had gone to prison. *What was she doing standing in the rain beside Mr Paterson? Surely she couldn't have used the tirthas?*

The thought of it made her feel sick, on so many levels. *What did it mean if the Kali priestess was in league with the Hoodoo priest?*

'Are you all right, child?'

She looked up and saw the worry in Lola's kindly face.

'Things… I…' she began. 'Things are serious,' she said. 'Things are really serious now…'

'Whatever it is you've seen, don't you worry, I'm here,' the woman whispered and gave her a sudden hug.

'What is it? Who's out there?' said Caroline.

'I think Miss Lizzie might have been right about Mr Paterson,' said Lola. Lizzie continued to press her cheek into the woman's chest, staring straight ahead at the bedroom wall.

'I never was sure about him,' said Caroline.

Bit late to admit it now, Lizzie thought vacantly.

There was a sudden frenzy of banging wood and smashing glass from downstairs. Lizzie pulled away from Lola's arms.

'Come on,' she said, as much to herself as the others. 'Caroline – you come with us to the top of the stairs. Get ready to throw everything you possibly can on the heads of anyone who comes up.

'Lola – you come with me downstairs and we'll go and see what we can do to keep them back. Here –' she passed the woman her rolling pin, 'use this if you have to.'

They went over and were about to lift Caroline up from the chair when the girl pushed them away.

'I think I can manage,' she said, with a little uncertainty in her voice.

They both watched as Caroline levered herself up with her elbows and then was standing upright, still clutching Sally Ally in one hand.

'Wow, will you look at you!' exclaimed Lola.

'It was all him,' said Lizzie. 'He's been sucking the life out of you for years. I bet you'll be fit as a fiddle in no time.'

If we survive the next few hours, she thought.

*

Lizzie and Lola left Caroline stationed at the top of the landing and crept down the stairs.

When they reached the hall all they could hear was the increasing cacophony of the plat eyes smashing at the shutters, as well as one or two just a few paces in front of them trying to break down the front door.

'They're not going to hold forever,' said Lizzie.

She was expecting the old *my wards'll hold 'em off* routine but when she glanced up at Lola she noticed a new solemnity in her expression. It made Lizzie suddenly nervous. *More* nervous.

'What is it?' she said.

'I gave him the Book.'

'What?'

'I gave it to him. I don't know why but I… I guess he must have somehow spelled me. It was… it was somethin' in his eyes. Somethin' hard to disobey, it seemed so natural to do it when he asked. Like giving it to him was of no consequence at all. I'm so sorry.'

Lizzie saw the tears in her eyes. *The woman was ashamed.* At first Lizzie was unsure how to act, embarrassed even, but then she knew. She stepped forward and put her arms around her waist.

'He's an evil man,' she whispered. 'But I promise – you and I, we will defeat him. Believe me.'

Lola sniffed, then drew back and held Lizzie's arms with both her hands. She smiled.

'We will,' she said. 'And we will protect Miss Caroline.'

At that moment there was a huge crash and they saw the shutters in the living room fly open.

'Quick!' said Lizzie and they ran down the hall towards the room.

Lizzie saw several arms come flailing in through the window and, as they reached the lounge, a leg swung over the window frame followed by a head of wiry hair with a great bushy beard.

Clunk!

Lola swiped the plat eye on the top of the head with the rolling pin. The creature cried out in pain and his arms came up to protect himself.

Clunk!

She struck one of the arms and the man scrambled out backwards on to the porch.

'Who's next?' shouted Lola.

Lizzie peeked out of the window and saw two other plat eyes standing alongside the first, evidently unsure about coming through.

Suddenly there was a crash from the far end of the hall. They looked round and saw that another set of shutters had been breached, and plat eye arms were thrusting through into the house.

'You stay here, I'll get them,' said Lizzie, and ran off down the hall leaving Lola brandishing the rolling pin as another plat eye ventured forward.

As Lizzie ran past the bottom of the stairs she looked up and saw Caroline propping herself on the upper banister.

'Lola's holding them off in the lounge!' she shouted. 'There's more coming in through the window by your room!'

'Do you want me to come down?' said Caroline.

'No, we're OK – you stay up there!'

But next thing Lizzie found herself skidding to a halt on the plush carpet as one of the plat eyes dropped down heavily in front of her from the window frame. It was the bald black man, the one who'd spotted her by the lagoon – and he didn't look at all happy. She snatched up one of the umbrellas, snapped it shut, and thrust it at him like a rapier.

'Get back!' she shouted. 'You're not wanted here!'

The man growled and lunged towards her.

She made as if to strike him in the face and then at the last moment jabbed downwards and hit him in the stomach.

The man doubled up with a gasp of pain, then stumbled and lost his footing. Lizzie was amazed to find him prostrate at her feet. Without thinking she grabbed the phone from the nearby table and bashed him repeatedly on the back of the head. It was only plastic, but after the third blow she was fairly sure she had knocked him out.

She hoped.

A loud cry – *a woman's cry* – made her spin round. Looking down the hall she saw that Lola was stumbling back from the living room window, away towards the fireplace and out of Lizzie's sightline. There was a plat eye lying prone on the floor – evidently one that Lola had knocked out – but there were two more now inside and the leader was… *Miles Day.*

With horror, Lizzie realised the problem. Lola's sense of servitude was ingrained. *No matter what the stake, she couldn't bring herself to fight the house's owner, her master.* Lizzie could hardly believe it.

She looked back and saw that someone was trying to get in through her own window. Quickly, she leapt forward and banged the shutters on to the plat eye's arms. Luckily he pulled his hands back, long enough for her to slam the shutters again and latch them. Then she ran down the corridor back into the lounge.

She froze in the doorway at the sight before her.

One of the plat eyes – the other one, not Miles – was standing over the fallen figure of Lola, who was facedown beside one of the large couches. The woman was not moving.

'What have you done to her?' screamed Lizzie and ran at the plat eye.

He turned and gazed at her with his vacant expression, distracting her entirely from Miles who had been standing by the door and who suddenly grabbed hold of her arm and yanked her towards him.

'No…' she gasped. Momentarily she was looking into his green eyes, behind the slightly crooked glasses – *what could she see there?* – and then he flung her sideways and she crashed into a small table with a pot plant.

But she sprang back up on to her feet, feeling surprisingly unhurt. She realised that she couldn't do anything against the two of them. *She had to retreat, to help Caroline as best she could now.*

'You…' she hissed at Miles. 'How could you let him do that to that woman who's been so loyal to you down the years?'

She was sure she caught a glimmer of remorse in those dull eyes as she turned and fled, back down the hall and up the stairs.

Chapter 17: The End of the Siege

'Where's Lola?' was the first thing Caroline asked as Lizzie pounded up the stairs.

'They've knocked her out,' said Lizzie, not knowing for one moment whether it was true. 'It's just you and me now.'

She picked up the two china storks and gave one to Caroline. 'When they come, let 'em have it. Don't show any sympathy, they don't deserve it.'

They stood there, both holding the birds up above their heads, ready to hurl them down on their assailants. But none came.

They heard clumping around downstairs, some banging and groaning.

'What are they doing?' said Caroline.

'No idea.'

More sounds of movement. *The tension was killing her.*

Then there was the sound of footsteps coming down the hall towards them from the living room. After a moment Mr Paterson and Lamya appeared, walking into view at a leisurely pace. At the bottom of the stairs they turned to look up at the two young girls. They were both drenched through.

It was Mr Paterson who spoke.

'You've done a magnificent job, ladies,' he said in his deep voice. 'But there's no point in fighting on any more. Just come down and we promise not to hurt you.'

'Don't say anything,' Lizzie whispered to her companion.

'Come on, do as Mr Paterson says,' said Lamya. 'We only want to talk to you. About the Book, and what you know about the tirthas.'

'What's a tirtha?' whispered Caroline.

'Tell you later.'

'They don't seem to be cooperating,' said Lamya, after a short pause. 'Cat got your tongues?' she called out.

Mr Paterson stepped up on to the first stair. He looked up at Lizzie. 'Now – you're not seriously going to tell me that if I come up to you, you're going to throw one of those birds at me, are you? They could really hurt, you know.'

Lizzie thought about that. It was true. Of course it would hurt. *But that was the idea!*

'You don't really want to hurt me, do you?' he said, taking another step up, and then another, all the time looking at Lizzie.

Of course she didn't really want to hurt him. But, if he kept on coming… she was going to have to.

175

Her arms were starting to ache, still holding the bird up above her head. She stared into the man's face, wondering when would be the best moment to throw.

'Come on now, I know you're a kind girl, Lizzie,' he said. 'Lola told me all about you…'

And he was up to the middle landing, coming closer. Could she really chuck a thing so heavy on someone's unprotected head? What if she killed him? *He obviously trusted her enough not to throw it...*

He trusted her. And trust was such a good quality. So much trust had disappeared from her life recently. She couldn't really throw it, could she, she didn't want to hurt him at all, she had never wanted to hurt anyone, it was only that that plat eye had scared the living daylights out of her, that's why she cut him, but she hated it, she hated doing it with all her heart, and she was full of revulsion when she hit the one just now on the head, wasn't she? And she had hated pushing Bakir down the ghat, and look where that had got him, no, she didn't want to hurt anyone ever again...

Then she glanced round at Caroline and saw the subdued look in the girl's dark eyes, the stork lying broken in two pieces beside her on the floor where she had dropped it.

A spell – *he was using magic on them!*

And when she looked back round he was only a few steps below her, Lamya a couple of steps behind him.

With all her might, she chucked the china bird at the top of Mr Paterson's head.

'Aah!' he cried as it struck his white cap with a horrible dull thud.

Lamya managed to catch the large man's wrist as he tumbled down the stairs, breaking his fall. Everything happened so fast that Lizzie momentarily lost the sense of it. But then Lamya was helping the stooped, wounded man back down towards the hall, shouting:

'Get them! Get them both! Now!'

And once again, the hall began to fill with plat eyes.

'There's too many of them!' cried Caroline.

'Don't panic,' said Lizzie. But as she saw them all jammed together down in the hall, pushing umbrellas out of the way and starting to mount the stairs she realised Caroline was exactly right. There *were* too many of them.

The teenage Afro-Caribbean boy with the particularly milky eyes was first up.

'Throw!' shouted Lizzie, and she and Caroline hurled the chair and floral lamp down at him.

The boy got his arms up in time to deflect the objects from his face but the force of them smashing into him knocked him backwards into the two men behind. One of those stumbled and fell over the side of the stairs, but managed to break what would have been a long fall by briefly catching hold of the banister as he dropped.

The other man steadied the bruised teenager and then they were both pushing on up the stairs, with many more surging behind them.

'Throw!' yelled Lizzie again, and this time a metal waste paper basket and a stone paperweight bounced off the oncoming plat eyes. The two leaders groaned and cried out, but kept coming. Lizzie saw that the man who had caught the teenager had a big cut on his forehead from where Caroline's paperweight had struck him.

Now there was only a heavy wooden footstool left.

'Go back in the bedroom!' shouted Lizzie, lifting it up. 'I'll catch you up.'

Caroline glanced at her uncertainly.

'Do it!' said Lizzie.

Suddenly Caroline leaned forward and kissed her on the cheek. 'Evelyn was right,' she said. 'You are a hero.'

And then she turned and limped back towards the Bird Room.

Caroline's words filled Lizzie with a renewed energy as she turned back to face the oncoming boys and men.

'This is going to really hurt, you know,' she said. 'Don't make me have to throw it.'

The teenage boy looked particularly uncertain, and the man beside him hesitated for a moment, but then the pressure from the plat eyes behind pushed them forwards up the stairs.

'OK,' said Lizzie, 'don't say I didn't warn you!'

And she hurled the stool with all her might down upon them. Without even watching to see what damage it had done – *she didn't particularly want to know* – she turned and ran back down the landing, catching Caroline round the waist halfway down and helping her the last few steps into the bedroom. As soon as they were inside she turned around and locked the door.

Lizzie looked at the bed. *Ideal, but way too heavy for the two of them to move.*

'Help me with the chair,' she said, and they pushed it over in front of the door just as the handle began to waggle loudly.

The two girls held each other for a moment, breathing raggedly.

When they drew apart, Caroline said: 'Out the window?'

'What about your illness?' said Lizzie.

'The adrenaline will keep me going.'

Lizzie looked at her uncertainly. 'You sure?'

Caroline nodded.

'OK then, let's try.'

As the plat eyes thumped and beat the panels and shook the handle of the door, the two girls hurried to the window and Lizzie flung it open. She looked out along the dark porch roof, which was still being pounded with rain.

'If only I hadn't broken that damned drainpipe last time,' Lizzie muttered. 'But there must be another one up the other side...'

'It looks slippery,' said Caroline.

'It is. But what else can we do?'

Suddenly there was an almighty bang followed by a cracking noise. Startled, they both looked round at the door and saw that an axe had broken through one of the panels, splintering the wood. They watched as it was levered and tugged and finally wrenched back out.

'God!' said Caroline.

'Look, I'll go first,' said Lizzie. 'Then I'll help you.'

She knew she had to test it first. *It had been easy to stand on the roof the first time round, but she had no idea how it would be in the rain – and the dark.*

There were several more blows on the door as she swung her legs out over the frame and prepared to lower herself on to the roof. She and Caroline kept fixing each other with looks, a feeble attempt to reassure themselves.

The door was breaking up fast now, Lizzie knew it wouldn't be long before the hoard was in.

'Here goes,' she said. Watched by Caroline, she let herself drop from the window ledge on to the sloping roof.

And immediately lost her footing and slipped.

Instinctively she twisted and tried to grab the ledge but somehow missed it. Next thing she knew she was sliding fast and uncontrollably down the wet roof, and then she was off over the edge and falling in the darkness.

She hit the ground and all went black.

*

It was very dark around the back of the house but luckily Pandu had got to know it reasonably well by now.

He felt his way carefully along the wall until he reached the study with its small glass-panelled door. His night vision wasn't bad, but the darkness out here in the countryside really was deep, with no street lighting to relieve it. *He knew there was a drainpipe around here somewhere.*

Eventually he found it and took hold of it with both hands. Luckily, with the house being so old, the pipe was an old-fashioned metal one, not one of those modern plastic ones which were likely to break. Hoping that he wouldn't wake Mr Tubs, he began carefully, slowly, to climb up.

Soon he was up past the study window and had reached the edge of a small section of tiled roofing that led to the bathroom window. If he could make his way up this without slipping, he could then use the frame of the window as a grip to get him to the edge of the wall of Lizzie's bedroom.

He was a good, confident climber, but it was so hard without being able to see anything properly.

With his left knee propped on the horizontal gutter, he leaned forward and probed the tiling with his fingers and palms. There was some moss, which worried him, as that made it more likely to slip. However he was pleased to find a few small, uneven gaps that he thought he could use for his fingers and toes.

He was going to have to really spread his weight out.

He thrust himself up, dug his fingers into two of the gaps, pressed the balls of his feet into the gutter, and spread himself flat.

Luckily, everything stayed in place.

He pushed himself upwards with his legs, still flat on his front.

There were a couple more gaps between the tiles beneath the bathroom window where he was able to wedge his fingers. Now he was fully spread-eagled across the small section of roof. He wondered how on earth he was going to stand up and get hold of the window frame.

By gambling, of course. He'd just seen his best friend torn to shreds, after all. *What did he care?*

With nothing to lose, he pushed himself off from the gutter with his feet, pushed himself up from the roof with his hands and hips, and propelled himself upwards with all the forward motion he could muster. His foot slipped and for a sliver of a second he thought he was going to fall but then somehow he was holding on to the window frame and pulling himself up closer, right up against the wall, his arms going out to the far sides of the frame so that he was flat up against the house, his feet teetering on tiptoes as he stabilised his balance.

He was OK.

He'd thought he was going to slip, he *had* slipped, but somehow as often happened in these situations he had managed to get a grip. He marvelled at how the body worked faster than the confused mind.

He shuffled sideways, keeping hold of the window edge – and then found a second downpipe on the jutting wall of Lizzie's bedroom. He was able to make a quick lunge to catch hold of that, then it was not too hard to reach round the corner and step on to the smaller ledge of tiling that ran beneath her window.

Within moments, he was standing flat against her window, straining his eyes to see into the bed which he knew was just below it.

For a moment he worried about how he was going to attract her attention without her waking up and screaming. Eventually he tried tapping the window very lightly. When nothing happened, he fumbled in his pocket and brought out his phone. He pressed the buttons and the screen lit up. He held it to the window, and shone it down on to her bed.

And saw that it was empty.

Chapter 18: L'il Xing

Stopping and looking back at herself, lying jumbled, hidden there in that bush – it was an afterthought, as much as anything.

But there was noise all about, all through the house behind her, so she turned and left behind her limp body with its upturned face, closed eyes, parted lips – and headed away across the lawn, past the toys, into the trees and marshy ground, lit as she went by her own inner light. Not that she needed it, because she knew where she was going.

As she left the din of the house behind she soon found herself in the darkness of the swamp. Rain splashed on the water, grass, and leaves all around her, and all around her she could sense many things that before had been occluded.

Most evident was the still shimmering waves and eddies of his magic, the incredible distortion he had managed to summon using the latent power of the tirtha to make his spell work – even without knowing its exact location. The magic was ebbing away now, but in many pockets and across lakes and trees shreds still remained, moving with curious ease like an oily rainbow on wet black tar. They were the final roils of the monstrous force he had used to prolong his longevity, to sate himself daily on the

184

regenerative power of the witchkin and of the Artefact of Power,
the humble manikin, that she cradled.

But beneath that there was much more. She sensed the
astonishing power of this place, neglected for aeons but known by
the ancients, with their reverence for the Great One, as well as by
the darker creatures that occasionally ventured forth from the
Opening, the shadow beings and those creatures whose hearts
flashed with light on the swamp at night, who would lead you
away to your doom.

The Opening was The One of The Many, and she made her
way to it directly, like a shimmer of filings to a magnet.

Within no time she was there. It may have been covered by
water in the mundane world, but she saw it as a great white-black
umbilical cord, twisting all around in the air and the swamp.
Wrapping in on itself as it arced back towards the heavens. A
Remnant of the Severing.

She walked forward and stepped into it.

*

Even in this hyper-sensual state, the place within the
tirthas was shadowy, mixed-up, akin to dream.

She heard children laughing at the edge of a sun-
dappled glade, a jester wailing in a tower, a ferocious
lizard roaring across a mountainside, dazzling nymphs
whispering and morphing into men with purple faces
and stubby horns, dogs with giant fangs barking and
chasing their tails, and a dull cacophony that
foreshadowed the end of all things in a not-so-distant
mystery...

185

It was as if she were on a roundabout that slowed every full turn to enable her a brief, focused glimpse of where she was.

With each revolution, amidst skeleton-priests, howling monkeys and bulbous-headed devils she saw a gap, a hole, a steadiness into which she knew she could step – or at least fall.

But the spinning, the swimming dynamism that she had experienced so many times before was altered slightly in this time. *Because of* his *residual magic,* she knew.

There were several options for her to focus on, to step forward into, this time. And whilst there was one, the obvious one, the needed one, there was also another in their midst that was intensely desired, no, not just desired, *needed* too, although the multitude of calculations required to understand why it was needed were not available in that jiggling, shaking, whirling place.

So she just stepped out into it, when it came round again.

*

She stepped out into a small mud clearing, surrounded by the lithe and snaking trunks of trees.

In front of her some of the trees had been felled, the startings of a path, but their slender stumps still remained. Behind her, a small, staked, waist-high sapling with variegated green-white leaves stood alone in the centre of the clearing.

She could sense the power – a great, primal power, so much greater than his *power – all around. This was The Nexus, the place where the Severing had happened.*

And she knew that she was in the right place, home, but that she was not in the right time.

It was the opportunity of a lifetime, and she walked out of the clearing, following the path of felled trees through the oak and ash forest.

Soon she came through a cast iron frame with a metal sun and moon at the top, which led into a larger area, one properly cleared and laid to lawn. Large beds planted with pink and red flowering bushes ran away down the sloping lawn, and beyond the small brook dividing the garden she could see the pink-washed, timbered flank of her home.

She walked through the wet grass, in between the beds, past a marble statue of a boy and then turned through a newly-planted, waist-high hedge into a small field with young fruit trees and a farm gate giving out on to the lane.

A boy was standing at the gate, holding a hoe, dressed in brown trousers and a dark blue shirt with a maroon scarf around his neck. He had a small white cap on his head, and he was staring at three boys on the other side of the gate, each stationary on a bike.

'Where'd you come from, Chinky?' shouted one of them.

'Off the ships at Bristol?' called another.

'Wouldn't you like to know,' replied the boy in the loose-fitting clothes. As she approached she saw his dark almond eyes, his Asian features.

She hurried forward and grabbed hold of the gate bars beside the boy.

'Scatter!' she shouted at the cyclists.

And they did, leaping up onto their saddles and pushing down hard on their pedals.

187

'Li'l Xing! Li'l Xing!' shouted one, looking over his shoulder. He was a handsome boy with a strawberry blond quiff and freckles.

'Get away with you, boy Barrow!' she yelled, and smiled.

The boy looked at her startled, then he was gone around the bend towards the front of the cottage.

The Chinese boy – for they were right, obviously, he was Chinese – turned and looked at her in wonder. After a few moments he smiled, and she smiled back at him.

'Pleased to meet you...?' he said.

'Lizzie,' she said. 'Lizzie Jones.'

'And you already know my name,' he said.

'Yes.'

'Do you want to see the owner of the house?' he said.

'I think so,' she said.

'This way.' He leaned the hoe against the gate and led her down past a potting shed crammed with dozens of plants in overspilling pots of compost, and across a large flat stone laid across the brook.

'You're doing a fantastic job,' she said.

'A flower cannot blossom without sunshine, nor a garden without love. We are, as I'm sure you know, doing something not just beautiful but very important here.'

She nodded, as they moved into the Sun Garden behind the house and then down the yew-hedged corridors which were already starting to bush out, evidently from an earlier phase of planting, past the Gothic Garden – she could see the freshly-carved statue of St Francis set by a metal chair – and the Easter Island Garden, without its wooden heads as yet, and finally on into the Indian Garden.

188

In the back area, past the rhododendron bush, a middle-aged woman with grey-blond hair was kneeling down and focusing intently on something. She evidently hadn't heard them coming up behind her.

'Evelyn,' said the boy.

The woman looked round sharply. She had a very distinguished face, with brown eyes, broad cheeks, and wide, pale lips. She was holding a small forked stick in her hands.

As she looked at the boy and his companion the sharpness faded and her eyebrows lifted.

'Oh...' said the woman.

'It's great to see it like this — the origins,' she said. 'You're a genius.'

'Thanks... thank you.'

There was a moment's silence, broken by the trilling of a blackbird.

'Miss Day is in danger,' she said. 'Or she will be. I'm Eric's great-niece, Lizzie. I'll do everything I can to help.'

The woman frowned. 'Oh — gosh. I... I think I understand,' she said.

She smiled, looked at Evelyn and Li'l Xing again.

'I must go now,' she said.

She turned her back on Li'l Xing and Evelyn and the flaring twisted green-black vortex of stars, worlds and blue-skinned gods that rose up right behind the kneeling woman.

*

She headed back across the brook, through the orchard, and down to the small clearing. At the freshly planted wedding cake tree, she stepped back into the mind-spinning dark-lightness of the tirtha.

Amidst the side-shuffling, drum-beating creatures with owl and buffalo and coyote heads and howls and shrieks and moons she held her focus, maintained her position in the maelstrom.

Soon the next right place swung round again.

Chapter 19: Pandu's Vision

What in Shiva's great name was he going to do now?

Pandu flashed the light from his phone about through Lizzie's window, unable to believe she wasn't there. What was he going to do? he wondered desperately again. Maybe she was sleeping in another room? *Or more likely staying over at a friend's.*

What terrible, terrible luck. As he began to make his way carefully back down the roof to the drainpipe, he considered his options. He could check out the other windows of the house. *No good, he'd either end up waking up Mr Tubs or having Lizzie's mum call the police because some peeping Tom was at the window.* He could head back to the village and try to find Ashlyn's house. *Just as hopeless.*

As he let himself fall the final metre to the ground, he realised that his best bet was to return to Kashi and hope that Sergeant Singh was still guarding the tirtha. At least the Sikh knew a little about the biggest secret on earth. Pandu would just have to hope there were no other police officers or civilians standing around to witness a boy appear out of nothing.

He began to walk across the dark Sun Garden, putting his hands out in front of him to ensure he didn't stumble into the bird bath that he knew was in the middle of the lawn. But just as his fingertips touched the rough stone structure he stopped, glimpsing light somewhere off to his right.

He looked around and saw a vague, silvery glow coming from the narrow path that led away past the end of the house down to the brook. The light vanished for a moment, then reappeared. Was someone coming with a torch?

What with the incredible strangeness of this garden he decided the best idea was to hide, as whoever it was appeared to be heading his way. He stumbled forward into the yew corridor, then crouched down and waited, watching.

Moments later, a ghost entered the Sun Garden.

As soon as he saw the creature, Pandu knew it was a ghost. It was almost transparent, human-shaped, with a bluish light shimmering all about it. His heart leapt in his throat as, after pausing for a few seconds, the ghost made its way straight across the lawn towards him.

Stifling a shriek, he scrambled backwards, thrusting his hands into the scratchy pitch black hedge to find the opening into the Gothic Garden. As soon as he felt the gap, he ran forward into the darkness until he stubbed his foot on the statue of the monk. Then he turned and crouched down in the corner, watching the darkness where he knew the opening to be. He tried to control his desperate breathing, tried to concentrate on something other than his lightning heartbeat, his immense fear.

The leaves on either side of the garden gateway began to glow with reflected light. Then the ghost stepped into the opening.

Pandu felt a frosty chill steal over him as the spirit walked forward into the small garden, coming closer and closer towards him. And then he realised. *It knew exactly where he was – and it was coming to get him.*

'Keep away from me!' he shouted as she – he saw now it had the face, the hair, the *shape* of a girl – came up in front of him, and bathed him in her electrical light.

Pandu.

He froze. Her mouth had moved, but there had been no sound – and yet he had clearly heard her say his name.

'Oh, Shiva save me...' he whispered. And then added: 'Lizzie?'

The ghost girl inclined her head slightly. He stared wide eyed at her features, the kinked nose, soft eyes, hair tied at the back in a pony tail.

'What... what happened?' he said.

Abruptly she turned her back to him, leaving one word echoing in his mind.

Follow.

*

What else could he do?

Today, his whole world had fallen apart. He had seen a woman ruthlessly slash a man's throat and a pair of monstrous dogs tear his closest friend to death. And now he was navigating the dark leafiness of a miraculous garden via the light of the ghost of his English girl friend. *Was everyone he knew and cared about dead?* Perhaps he had died too without realising it, maybe falling from the cottage roof, and now he was being led away to heaven.

He could hardly comprehend it and so walked quietly behind the ghost girl, as if in a trance.

They crossed the brook, headed past an outhouse, through a small field with trees, across another open garden area, and then passed under a frame at the top of which Pandu briefly noticed a metal sun and moon, reflecting the half-light of the spirit's aura. They went down a narrow hedge-lined path and came through a gate into an overgrown garden with a single large tree in the centre. Here, the ghost of Lizzie stopped and ushered him forward with a wave of her hand.

He moved right up close to her, his face rigid with disbelief and confusion. She glowed, white and dark and pearl and silver, some features, her eyes and mouth particularly, and her clothes, quite clear, but others just a space into the darkness behind her. And he *felt* her, felt a charged, electrical pressure brushing against his face in waves, but he also felt something more – the presence of her personality, her essence, of the laughter and courage and determination that was Lizzie at her core – and he was overwhelmed by her and tears began to blur his eyes.

Hold it.

He looked down to where she was pointing and saw a small, soil-stained doll at the foot of the tree. Without thinking, he reached down and grasped it.

Now hold the tree.

*

And he was there, in the maelstrom, spinning round in the vortex, seeing lights exploding, chisel-faced men with black hair adorned with feathers dancing around poles, screeching birds, alligators hissing and twisting on themselves as they opened their great jaws, lights sucking out the souls of young women, daggers with blood, a laughing dog, squawking crow, the patting of drums, and all the while he was close to her, within the protective power of her spirit, safe from the chaos and harm, from the awful beauty and fabulous terror of this space, until suddenly he was cold and wet and sucking down water and his eyes were wide open in watery darkness and he was panicking and thrusting himself forward and backward and sideways until eventually he came out into dry air, choking, choking and crying...

*

She was kneeling over him, looking into his eyes as he stared blankly up. He saw the deep care, the total concern for him, in her face and for a moment he almost wished he were dead and that this was heaven. The world was too harsh, violent and unfair. He wanted for one moment to be free of it – and he was, here, now, in her eyes.

But she was a ghost.

He sat up, pulling himself back from her, startled again by the unreality of the flickering being before him.

'Are you dead?' he asked.

No.

She stood up and began to move away into what he now saw was a vast, moonlit marsh interspersed with large, shadowy trees.

Come.

He started to follow her, and next thing he was up to one of his knees in sloppy mud. He sat down abruptly, pulling his leg out.

Be careful. Follow me carefully.

'I hear you,' he said, raking his hair with his fingers, scarcely able to believe her voice was echoing in his head.

And so they made their way through the bayou, the gangly, soaked-through Indian boy led by the sparkling, half-gone ghost girl.

The complexity of navigating each footfall thankfully kept the potentially overwhelming feeling of despair from Pandu's thoughts. A light rain was falling in fits and starts, and a faint breeze cooled him slightly, but he could sense that the air was very warm and humid here. He wondered where they were. He knew Lizzie had discovered another tirtha besides the Kashi one, and that Ashlyn's reading of Eric's journals seemed to describe many more. He could be anywhere. Anywhere in the world. *Or even anywhere in another world.* Fleetingly, he hoped that the spirit leading him deep into this unknown country was genuinely Lizzie, and not some malicious *bhoot* aiming to trick him. He glanced down at her feet and saw they faced the right way, unlike a bhoot's which were supposed to face backwards – or so his mum had told him.

I'm going crazy, he thought, as he weaved in between the dark trunks of trees whose branches were draped in long, tangled mosses that looked like spider web in the ghost's half-light. He imagined becoming trapped and a huge black spider rushing out to poison him with a bite and wrap him up in her deadly silk.

Suddenly the spirit stopped.

She turned to face him, and her mouth moved urgently.

I must go. Keep on that way.

She pointed a way through the swamp. And vanished.

'No!' shouted Pandu. 'Don't leave me...'

But it was too late. The creature was gone. Leaving him alone in the dark swamp.

For a moment his panic blinded him. All he could see by the faint light of the moon was the ghastly trees with their shaggy coats of moss, and the treacherous black pools of water.

And then he looked the way she had pointed and saw a light. A proper light.

Was it a house?

Grabbing up a stick to test his way, he began to hurry on through the marsh. After a short while the trees thinned and he saw that indeed it was a house, a large house with lights on and a sloping roof and a kids' slide and paddling pool on the rough grass in front of it. He ran forward, past caring if he was in danger.

As he came towards the porch of the great house he saw that the front door was open and several of the windows had been smashed. But there didn't seem to be anyone around. He climbed up the small flight of steps on to the porch, and looked in through the front door.

'Hello?' he said, cautiously. 'Is anyone there?'

Someone groaned and he looked around. *It didn't sound like it had come from inside the house.*

'Hello?' he said again.

'Help,' said a small voice. He strode along the porch and looked over the balcony into the bushes below. Someone was in there, moving around.

'Who is it?' he said.

'Pandu? Is that you?'

'Lizzie!'

He ran back to the steps and then around to the bush. He thrust away dense, springy branches and grabbed her by the arms.

'Are you OK?' he said, pulling her up and out.

'I... I think so,' she said. Her hair was dishevelled and she was standing slightly crookedly. 'My knee hurts,' she added.

'You've cut your arm,' he said, smudging the blood with his finger.

And suddenly they were hugging each other tightly.

'I'm so glad to see you,' she said into his ear. 'How did you get here?'

'You... it was you... your spirit... it was you, wasn't it?'

'What?' she said, pulling back from him, smiling, holding the sides of his arms.

'You came and got me. Your spirit... how did you do it?'

'Do what?'

'You... you don't remember?'

Lizzie thought. 'I remember slipping off the roof...' And suddenly it all came back to her.

'Caroline...' she said, turning back towards the house. 'Lola!' she shouted and ran up the steps into the house. Pandu ran after her, down the hallway with its curious scattering of broken umbrellas and smashed ornaments, on into a beautiful but overturned room where he saw Lizzie already kneeling down beside the form of a woman.

By the time he'd got to her she was looking up at him, tears streaming from her eyes.

'She's dead!' she said.

'What?' he knelt down and slowly turned the woman over. Her eyes were closed, and she looked peaceful.

'What happened?' he said, feeling swiftly at the woman's neck and wrist, trying to find a pulse.

'We were attacked by plat eyes and Mr Paterson and... that awful priestess. Lamya, that was her name, wasn't it?'

'Lamya!' Pandu cried. 'I've just seen her – in Hebley, in a big house – she was with another man and these awful beasts. Lizzie – Lizzie – they killed Raj!'

'No...'

'We followed her from Kashi, through your garden, down to a large, empty house in the village. When we went down into the basement we were attacked by her and a Chinese man, and they had these terrible dogs. It was awful... I had to run...'

They both fought back their tears.

'There's no time now,' said Lizzie. 'Look – you see if there's anything you can do to try and revive her – I have to go upstairs, there was someone else we were with.'

'Is it safe?'

'Nothing's safe anymore,' said Lizzie. 'It just has to be done.'

And she ran out of the room, leaving Pandu to try and resuscitate the poor, prostrate form of Lola.

A few minutes later she was back. She saw immediately from the look on Pandu's face that he had been unable to do anything for the woman.

The plat eyes had killed Lola.

She could hardly believe it, she felt like her anger would make her explode. Her grief would have to wait.

'Come on,' she said, pulling Pandu up. 'There's nothing we can do for her now. But we have someone else to save. Follow me.'

And Pandu, grateful that he'd heard her voice normally this time, followed Lizzie once more.

Chapter 20: The Ritual at the Lagoon

With one blow from his dagger the man severed the cockerel's neck and let the blood pour down over the girl's head. He grinned happily as she screamed.

'You ancestors, you Papa Parson spirit and you James Headley spirit and you Sister Jessica spirit, you take the washing of this girl's head with this bird's blood as final purification of her sweet innocent soul for you...'

It was difficult for Lizzie and Pandu, crouched in scrub near the clearing, to hear what he said next because Caroline began screaming again as the cockerel's pumping blood matted down her blonde hair and streamed in rivulets down her pale cheeks.

'What in Shiva's name are we going to do?' whispered Pandu.

There were at least a dozen plat eyes standing around in the clearing, watching as their master carried out his grotesque ritual. Caroline was tied up around her waist against the ancient oak tree. Lamya stood next to Mr Paterson, who was now wearing a black suit and had painted his face grey, making him look like a ghoul. *A ghoul in a flat white cap.*

The clearing was lit by dozens of black candles, carefully set out on the ground and nestled in the branches of adjacent trees. Two large iron candelabras had been positioned on either side of the central tree, their candles flickering in front of the dusky, moonlit surface of the lagoon. Beside one candelabra was the empty cage of the rooster, and a second cage with another chicken. Beside the other was a cage containing at least three dark, intertwined snakes.

It was to this cage that Mr Paterson turned after shaking the last of the bird's blood out over Caroline's face.

'These darlings here will... *enable* this Conjure of Sacrifice,' he said, reaching down to lift the cage. Lizzie noticed Lamya's dark eyes flash in the candlelight as she looked around at the plat eyes, gormlessly watching the spectacle unfold before them. The priestess was clutching something in her hands, playing with it, twisting it around – *it was the painted manikin, Sally Ally!* Lizzie was surprised by the expression on Lamya's face... was it worry? *Or fear, even?*

A hushed silence fell over the strange crowd, and all the plat eyes stood stock still.

'We have to do something now,' Lizzie whispered. 'I think he's going to kill her!'

'What?'

'I don't know!'

Having sheathed his dagger, Mr Paterson opened the cage. Lizzie winced to see one of the snake's heads strike out and bump against his hand.

'It's bitten him!' hissed Pandu.

'Ah yes, you will do nicely, my lovely,' said Mr Paterson, and he snatched the snake by its head and lifted it out of the cage. Lizzie could see blood pouring down the back of his hand.

'He's not human,' she whispered. 'Not *normal* human, anyway...'

Caroline was staring in horror as Mr Paterson raised the snake towards her. The other two snakes quickly escaped from the cage and slithered across the clearing, in between the candles and the plat eyes' feet. They disappeared beneath the wheels of Mr Paterson's truck, parked a short distance away.

'We've got to move *now*,' said Pandu.

'Yes!'

'But what are we going to do?'

'Still don't know!' shouted Lizzie, although she did have the start of an idea.

Several things happened at once. The two teenagers leapt out from the scrub and ran into the clearing. Lizzie saw Mr Paterson thrust the snake, jaws stretched wide and fangs bared, at Caroline's face – only to be knocked sideways by Lamya just before the creature could strike.

'What...' he began, staring bewildered at the priestess whilst still clutching the snake. But Lamya had already spun away from him and was pulling her dagger from

203

her belt as she heard the teenagers running towards them. The plat eyes began to groan.

Pandu launched himself at the priestess.

'You killed Raj and Bakir!' he yelled, just managing to twist in the air as she slashed at him. He collided with her, and they both crashed down into the mud at the water's edge. Sally Ally was thrown clear, landing near Caroline's feet. Lamya was winded by the blow and Pandu used the moment to grab hold of her knife hand and bang her wrist against the old tree root, knocking the blade out of it.

Meanwhile, Lizzie veered back from Mr Paterson as he thrust the snake's open jaw and fangs straight at her face.

'Get her!' he shouted at the plat eyes.

Lizzie glanced around, saw a mass of hollow-eyed men and boys stretching out their hands for her. She dived low but a hand caught her pony tail and yanked her backwards. She screamed, and within moments strong hands had grabbed her arms and legs. She struggled and tried to kick but couldn't free herself. She noticed the bespectacled face of Miles, leering as he grasped her leg, and the young boy Hector holding on to her right foot.

'Pull her apart!' shouted Mr Paterson.

'No!' shouted Caroline, and he turned and struck her across the face.

'Time to finish you off,' he said, lifting the diamond-patterned snake that was still coiling and writhing in his other hand. He thrust it towards Caroline's face.

'Look, you fool, he is going to KILL YOUR SISTER!' Lizzie yelled at Miles.

Pandu was still struggling with Lamya, feeling again the priestesses' surprising strength and agility that he'd first experienced in the Kali temple. She had managed to force her way out from underneath him so now both were on their knees, slipping and grappling on the bank of the lagoon. She dug her nails into his cheeks, forcing his head backwards so he was leaning out over the water.

'Help!' Lamya shouted, and over her shoulder Pandu could see plat eyes advancing.

'I hate you!' he yelled.

Lamya pushed him further out, blood streaming in his eyes from the gashes of her nails. He would have gone into the lake but for the fact that one of the plat eyes had grabbed hold of his shin, and was tugging him back towards the clearing.

He kicked hard back and the creature's grip loosened briefly, enough for him to kick again and free his leg. He saw Lamya's dark eyes flick to her left, down at the knife at the base of the oak tree and he realised she was planning to make a lunge for it.

Just as she did, he roared and used all his remaining strength to thrust her in the same direction she was lunging. He caught her by surprise, and she flew towards the knife much faster than she'd realised. Her head struck the tree beside it with a hard crack, and she slumped down.

Pandu's momentary elation was curbed by the three plat eye men bearing down on him.

Meanwhile, with her limbs being pulled in all directions, Lizzie realised with horror that the plat eyes were doing exactly as their master had commanded them – they were literally trying to tear her apart. She screamed, and then noticed that her right leg had been released. Her foot came down on the ground, and she tried desperately to position herself to reduce the pain of the stretching by the plat eyes who still held her.

She looked towards the oak tree, hoping that her desperate plan had worked.

'Stop!'

Mr Paterson froze at the sound of the man's voice, the snake's fangs inches away from Caroline's stricken face. He looked around, the candles casting shadows across the ghastly grey paint on his cheeks and forehead.

A fist came up swiftly and struck the bottom of his jaw. Mr Paterson staggered backwards, releasing hold of the snake which twisted and coiled in the air. It slapped the ground and writhed away. Miles advanced quickly on the tall man and struck him hard in the face again.

'You will not... *harm* her,' hissed the plat eye.

'Don't tell me what to do. You are my slave!' shouted Mr Paterson.

Miles leapt forward and grabbed hold of him around the chest, propelling him backwards. There was a loud splash as they both fell into the lagoon.

Lizzie felt the pressure on her limbs ease, and suddenly she was sitting on the ground, released by the remaining plat eyes who had with their fellows walked up to the bank of the lagoon. Seeing that Pandu appeared to be all right beside the prone figure of Lamya, she hurried over to Caroline and quickly used the priestess' knife to cut the girl free.

Caroline immediately snatched up her doll, Sally Ally, that had landed near her feet when Lamya fell. Then she clutched Lizzie in a brief embrace before they both turned around to watch the strange spectacle unfolding before them.

The plat eyes were all stood in a line watching quietly as Miles, eyes alight with savagery, and Mr Paterson struggled in the shallow water at the lagoon's edge.

'Help me, you idiots!' Mr Paterson was shouting. 'Help, get him off me!'

But they didn't respond as Miles got the upper hand and, holding the tall man by the lapels of his suit, thrust him back and down into the dirty water. Mr Paterson's head went under but his hands came up and tried to push the plat eye back. But Miles, although clearly a delicate man, was possessed of a supernatural strength and with iron force held the much larger man down.

Like Caroline, Lizzie had to turn away, although she saw that Pandu remained watching until the bitter end, when the sound of splashing and struggle finished. After a while, there was a softer sound of water swishing as Miles walked out of the lagoon.

Alone.

Chapter 21: Miles' Story

'We were all just ordinary men and boys, our souls held captive by the malevolent, long dead spirits of the bayou driven into us by Paterson.'

Driving the truck on the way back to Cypress House, a traumatised but lucid Miles was telling them all he knew in his refined Southern accent. Caroline was sitting in the front, holding on to his side, whilst Lizzie and Pandu were in the back.

'It was torture, being imprisoned in our own minds by his potions and his Hoodoo. We've been like this for years, ever since he set up the time magic. But whilst Paterson knew how to make a plat eye, he didn't know what it was like to *be* one. He never realised that each of us was still a human being inside, bated daily by our evil possessors, and by the knowledge that we could do nothing except obey his tyrannical orders. We did everything we could to reassert control over ourselves, but it was impossible.'

He drew in a sharp breath through clenched teeth as he continued: 'Lola was terrible, seeing her hurt was like being cut across my heart. But then, when I realised he was going to kill you, Sis – well, there came up such an almighty storm of rage inside me that I was finally able to rid myself of the perverse homunculus sitting on my soul all these years.'

'But how did it all begin? What was Mr Paterson trying to do?' asked Lizzie, watching past Miles and Caroline as the headlights swept against the dark trees.

'He chatted to us all the time about his plans, never stopped. I guess he thought we'd be his slaves forever – or at least until it was too late to do anything to stop him.

'He found out about the tirtha and the Book from our older brother who was killed in the War. I'm not sure how, but it led him to here. He never told me he'd met Henry. I gave him the grocery contract because he seemed –' Miles sneered '– he *seemed* a decent sort.

'But all the while he was plotting. Plotting to take me out, to infest ordinary, decent folk with plat eye spirits under his control and plotting to... *feed*... off you indefinitely, Sis, by suspending everything in a pocket of time.'

For a moment Miles went silent, his eyes fixed grimly on the road. Caroline, whose blood-stained cheeks were already streaming with tears, let out a small wail.

'No one will hurt us again, Sis,' Miles whispered. 'Ever.'

He took a deep breath and continued: 'With Hurricane Carla approaching he saw his moment. When I drove off to get emergency supplies he used magic to crash a tree on the car. When I woke up I was tied to a table in his barn. He force fed me his disgusting potions, full of blood and worse, and over a period of several days he broke me down with chanting and by conjuring terrifying visions in my head. After a while it was too much and I lost my mind. When I next grew conscious there was something awful inside me, controlling me, and all I could do was submit to it. And look on in horror at the things it made me do.'

His voice cracked as he spoke the last few words. Lizzie leaned into Pandu, who put his arm around her.

'How did he freeze time?' she asked.

'I don't know,' said Miles. 'More Hoodoo. We spent days carving out these runes in a wide circle around the bayou, whilst he was working his magic in the barn. He talked about drawing power from the portal though thank God he – and we – never found it.

'After we'd finished, that one single day in September 1961 just kept repeating – although we who were living through it still retained some sense of continuity, however impaired. Then he began his feeding off your blood, Sis. Our main orders were to make sure you and Lola didn't leave the house. Besides that, we spent our time searching for the tirtha – thankfully Dad never told me exactly where it was, and it's good and hidden, deep in a pool. After a while he told us to give up. He used more of his witchcraft to make Lola reveal the location of The Book of Life and then give it to him – although that frustrated him too, as he couldn't decipher its meaning. I think it's written in some ancient oriental language, Mandarin or something. At first he thought I might know something about it but soon realised I didn't.'

The truck's headlights lit up the side of Cypress House.

'Then everything changed when the Polish woman turned up. *Eva.*'

'Who?' Lizzie said, her skin crawling. She looked at Pandu.

'Eva. Eva Blane. Paterson was *really* taken by her. She'd come through from the tirtha, and knew about the Book. They hatched some scheme together – Paterson was excited and agreed to let Eva take the Book back through the tirtha with her. After that, he was much more agitated. He talked about Eva all the time – oh, and he started mentioning your old Indian doll, then, Sis – Sally Ally, isn't it? He said he'd always liked that doll, but now he realised its importance, too.'

Caroline frowned, clutching Sally Ally even tighter to her side as if she would never let her go again.

'And then things upped a gear when first the Chinese man and then you came through, Lizzie,' Miles continued. 'Followed a few days later by the Indian priestess. Paterson decided he could stop the time magic, and do without your blood anymore, Sis – although he still talked about needing to keep some for something else,' he said, shuddering briefly and glancing at Caroline. 'By killing you in that Hoodoo ritual he could do the Conjure of Sacrifice, an ancient spell which would take all your remaining years away and transfer them to him.'

'We know the Polish woman – and the Chinese man,' said Pandu grimly.

'You do?' said Miles.

'Yes. She's a demon, who we killed in... well, through another tirtha. It's a long story. And the Chinese guy was doing something with the Book, with the priestess and some other guy – an Englishman – in the cellar of a house back in Hebley. My Uncle Raj and I followed the priestess and overheard them talking. I think... yes, I'm *sure* they mentioned your brother, Henry – and a doll too. That must be the one,' said Pandu, looking at Sally Ally. 'I think they said it was some kind of artefact...'

A shadow crossed his face. 'But then they heard us and... and they had these dogs, which turned into monsters and... they killed Raj...'

Lizzie looked up at his blood-stained face in the darkness. For a moment she was scared by the anger she saw there.

An anger which hadn't been assuaged by killing Lamya.

'We have to go back,' she said, as the truck drew up in front of the house. 'We have to find Raj, and get the Book.'

*

They left Miles to look after Caroline and deal with the burial of Lola, which he said he would do with the other men now freed from Mr Paterson's power. He said they would also bury Lamya, and fish the Hoodoo priest's body out of the lagoon and put him in the ground too. But how they would re-establish their lives in a new century, neither he nor Caroline knew. It was all too much to consider now, they would just deal with one thing at a time. Lizzie promised to come back through the tirtha and talk to them again soon, and she said she would bring her Wiccan friend Ashlyn who could surely help too.

Before they left Cypress House, Lizzie went up to Lola's body in the living room. She knelt down beside her.

'I will never forget your bravery,' she said, tears welling in her eyes. 'Without you, I would never have been able to cope with all this.'

She leaned forward and kissed her cheek, stifling a sob. Then she stood up and turned round to see Pandu, standing in the doorway.

'Come on,' he said. 'We need to go.'

And, unlike Lizzie, he remembered the way back.

Chapter 22: The Book of Life

'So you're trying to tell me you can't remember it *at all?*'

'No,' said Lizzie.

She was trudging, cold and wet, with Pandu towards the village across the dark, silent fields. It had been weird to walk straight past her house where she knew her mum and Mr Tubs were still sleeping soundly. But at least now she knew – *to her huge relief* – that, as Pandu had confirmed, only a few hours had passed since she went through the tirtha, instead of all the *days* she had lived through in Louisiana. At least there was something to be grateful for from the time hex.

'But you were there, right in front of me in the garden, like a ghost! You told me – or *telepathically* told me – to follow you!' said Pandu.

'That's ridiculous.'

'Come on, how else would I ever have known where you were?'

Lizzie was unable to reply. She was convinced she hadn't known anything at all whilst she was unconscious. *But then...*

'Let's leave it for now,' she said. 'We've got something far more urgent to deal with. Tell me exactly what happened right from the beginning in Kashi. We've got time before we get to Ashlyn's.'

And so he explained to her everything that had happened since he first overheard Lamya talking to Sabi with the Englishman in the Marble Palace. By the time he'd finished they were nearing Limetree Cottage, the house in the woods on the outskirts of Hebley where Ashlyn lived.

'What time is it?' asked Lizzie.

It was only then that Pandu found his phone had been ruined by its soak in the bayou.

'If you came through some time after one it must be the middle of the night now,' said Lizzie. Suddenly a dreamlike image of the swamp and weird swirls of bluish light flitted across her mind. 'That is, if time's working right now, of course,' she added uncertainly.

'Whatever time it is, the lights are still on,' said Pandu.

As they came down alongside the bulging garden hedge they could hear voices coming from the house. They were quite loud.

'Sounds like they've been drinking,' said Lizzie.

'Or they're arguing,' said Pandu.

'Or both.'

As they came in the gate and approached the door they could see into the small living room, where the window was open and Ashlyn was talking to the elderly witch, Madeline, whom Lizzie had also first seen at Godwin Lennox's hunt. She remembered with a shudder how the smarmy businessman – with whom

215

her mum was now so close – had swung his whip at the old lady.

'... we can't use that magic anymore,' Ashlyn was saying. 'It's not safe. You just have to accept...'

'I don't have to accept anything,' said Madeline. 'I've asked for the coven's help. It's healing I need, nothing more, nothing less.'

'But it's not healing when the recipient is... when they're aging... *naturally*,' said Ashlyn, and then she heard the teenagers outside and looked out of the window. 'Lizzie!' she cried.

Within moments Lizzie and Pandu were ensconced in the sitting room, with Madeline hurrying about to make them hot cocoa and bring dry clothes. At first Lizzie was concerned to sense an awkward atmosphere between the two Wiccans, but it soon disappeared as they helped clean her and Pandu up, and when she began to tell them the bizarre outline of what had happened.

'I'll tell you the full story tomorrow,' she said. 'What Pandu has to say is the most important, as we have to do something right now – tonight. Something very dangerous. And... and, Pandu – Raj...'

Madeline put her arm around her as she suddenly started crying, as did Ashlyn with Pandu when she saw how distraught he was too.

'What's happened?' said Madeline.

'Lamya got freed on bail,' said Pandu. 'She's dead now – that's another story – but earlier today, Raj and I came through the tirtha and discovered her with a couple of other people in the basement of a house in the village. And they had dogs which turned into these awful *monsters* – and they... they *killed* Raj! I... I had to run. I feel so terrible!'

'Don't worry, you did what you had to,' said Madeline, holding his face against her shoulder.

'Where was the house?' said Ashlyn.

'Down near the church.'

'On the lane running up to it?' said Ashlyn.

'Yes,' said Pandu.

'On the left or the right, as you're approaching the church?' said Ashlyn.

Lizzie saw the look of deadly concern on Ashlyn's face. Suddenly it dawned on her.

'Eva's house...' she said.

They all looked at each other. It was Ashlyn who finally broke the silence.

'Let's go,' she said. 'You can tell us everything else we need to know on the way.'

*

The gate into the Manor house garden from the churchyard was still ajar when they reached it. It was Pandu who got there first, and peered around the edge.

'No one about,' he said.

They filed through, past the pond and on to the back door. Pandu tried the handle and found to his surprise that it was still open.

'Perhaps Chen Yang left it open expecting Lamya back,' said Lizzie. She was sure the man Pandu described was the same man Godwin had employed as their gardener, who had also been at Lady Blane's party last year.

'Be really quiet,' whispered Pandu. 'We've got to surprise those dogs before they change.'

They had all brought pairs of Ashlyn's socks with them and proceeded to put them over their shoes to muffle them on the hard, wooden floorboards. Then they entered the house, holding hands as Pandu led them through to the kitchen and the door that went down to the basement. The house was absolutely still and quiet, and it was hard for the teenage boy to see where he was going. A few times he had to put his hands out in front of him to make sure he didn't collide with all the kitchen units and tables and chairs that he knew were there.

As he reached the cellar door there was a sudden clunk from somewhere behind him. He spun round and peered at the shuffling, dark figures.

'Sorry,' whispered Madeline. 'It was me – just found something that might help us.'

Pandu slowly turned the handle. He pushed the door open and was relieved to see that there was still a light on in the corridor below, so they wouldn't need to use their torches.

Slowly, they descended the stone steps down into the narrow, musty corridor. Pandu saw that the doors on the right and left were still shut. The one at the far end – where the dogs and people had come out from last time – was fractionally open. A light – probably just a small lamp – was on in there.

He turned and gestured urgently at his companions, pointing at the open doorway. He'd briefed them about the layout on their walk from Ashlyn's cottage to the Manor house, so they knew what he meant and followed him stealthily down the corridor. They reached the door and Pandu looked in through the crack.

The dogs were asleep, lying in two large baskets against the wall. They were in their normal, Spaniel form. Pandu couldn't see anything – or *anyone* – else in that part of the room.

He pulled the heavy spanner out of his pocket and turned round to the others, who were similarly producing their homemade weapons. Then he raised his hand and counted down with his fingers – *three, two, one...*

He pushed the door open and the four of them charged into the room.

The dogs woke as the humans rushed at them, their faces quickly transforming into ferocious snarls. The first leapt up, its body bulging with sudden, unnatural growth, but Pandu struck it with his spanner and knocked it backwards. Ashlyn forced the second back with a blow from her long staff. Its eyes swirled into lurid yellow-green as it spun round and began growling and snapping at her. But before they knew it, someone had leapt between them and with two quick blows both dogs were lying motionless on the ground, in a pool of their own blood.

Pandu looked round at the assailant and saw to his amazement that it was Madeline. He realised what the old woman had picked up from the kitchen – a large cleaver.

Madeline had drops of blood spattered on her face. She looked drained, but pleased with herself.

'Spotted it on one of the counters,' she said. 'Eaten carrots all my life!'

'Look!' shouted Pandu.

They all turned and saw that the young Chinese man – Lizzie was right, it *was* Chen Yang – had leapt up from a small bed and was running in his pyjamas towards the door. He had a large book clutched under his arm.

Lizzie was closest to him and rushed to block his path. She swung a large metal serving spoon at him but he easily ducked it and shoved her aside. She stumbled backwards, but just managed to keep her footing.

Ashlyn hurled her staff at Chen Yang and it struck him in the ribs, causing him to cry out in pain – but he kept running. Then Pandu crashed into him and the two slammed into the door. Chen Yang dropped the book and kicked out at the teenager, who was trying to grab his arms. Pandu let out a howl as the man's knee jabbed into his stomach. The Indian was forced to let go of the man, who in the next moment was racing away down the corridor.

'I'll go after him!' shouted Ashlyn. 'You lot stay here and check the other rooms in case there's anyone else around.' She ran off down the passage.

Madeline and Lizzie went over to Pandu who was sitting on the floor, clutching his stomach and gasping.

'Are you OK?' said Lizzie.

'Yes... he just... winded me,' said Pandu. 'He'd better... not... get away,' he added, and then let out a stream of curses in Hindi.

Lizzie looked around the room. It had no windows and was sparsely furnished, with just the single bed, a table and two benches. On the table a plate with a spoon was smeared with the remains of a brown sauce, evidently Chen Yang's supper. A small lamp stood beside it.

'Come on, let's check the rest out,' said Madeline, and Lizzie went down the corridor with the witch, checking out each of the other doors. Before opening each one, they stopped and listened against it.

The first door opened into a storeroom filled with tools and electrical equipment. The second was a larger room marked out with a giant circle on the floor, chalked up with elegant, strange shapes and the figures of animals and people. There was a waist height stone block in the centre of the circle. It was draped in black cloth, in the middle of which stood an inverted bronze cross. Elaborate candelabras stood in each corner, their black iron fingers thickened by the melted wax of countless white candles.

'Something for rituals, black magic I suspect,' said Madeline, moving carefully around the circle. Lizzie was walking past her towards the makeshift altar, when Madeline's hand grabbed her shoulder.

'Don't go in the circle,' she said. 'There's a bad vibe in here.'

By the time they reached the final door, Pandu had properly recovered and joined them. When Lizzie listened, she heard a strange moaning on the other side of the door. She shuddered, remembering the plat eyes groaning out on the bayou at night.

'Someone's in there,' she said.

They readied their makeshift weapons. Pandu turned the handle and pushed the door, but it stuck on the uneven stone floor so he had to push it harder, cursing that they'd lost the element of surprise.

He cried out as the door opened fully and Lizzie rushed forward, wielding her spoon. But as soon as she saw the room's occupant she stopped dead in her tracks.

'Raj!' she cried.

The Inspector was sitting propped up in the corner, bruised and bloody. His uniform was torn and dirty, his shoes had been removed, and he was chained around his ankle to the wall. But his eyes, puffy as they were, opened when he heard his name.

'Lizzie...' he gasped.

'Uncle – you're alive!' cried Pandu, rushing up to him.

'And... thank Shiva... so are you!' said the Inspector.

'I thought you were dead,' said Pandu, tears of relief in his eyes.

'So did I,' said Raj. His lips shook and Lizzie realised he was trying to smile, but he was so black and blue he could scarcely move.

'What happened?' said Pandu, checking the chain.

'The priestess was coming to finish me off… when the Chinese guy shouted… and she stopped. He persuaded her… to keep me alive… in case they couldn't find you. Obviously they didn't know… how much we knew… about the tirthas… and what they're up to. I suppose… they might have been worried… that the whole Uttar Pradesh police force… knew about them…

'So it was your skilful escape… that kept me alive, Pandu. I knew… I could count on you.'

The boy threw his arms around the Inspector, who cried out in pain. Pandu drew back quickly.

'Sorry, Uncle,' he said.

'How bad are you hurt?' said Lizzie.

'They didn't torture you, did they?' said Pandu, remembering the horrible wounds that Lamya had inflicted on Bakir in the basement of the Kali temple.

'No, not yet,' said Raj. 'That's one thing to be grateful for. But I feel very weak and… the pain is great, particularly… in my chest… and arm.'

Pandu looked at the wounds. They were horribly bloody, and the torn skin had a yellow-green hue.

'It's where those creatures bit him,' he said quietly to Madeline as he stood up.

'The wounds look nasty,' she said grimly.

Suddenly there was a noise in the corridor outside and Lizzie rushed to the door.

'It's Ashlyn!' she said.

'I lost him,' said the auburn-haired witch, as she came into the room. Her anger quickly turned to elation – and then to concern – as she saw the Inspector.

'Raj - what did they do to you?' she said, kneeling down beside him.

'Duffed me up bad,' said Raj. His attempt at a laugh sent him into a coughing fit, which had both Pandu and Ashlyn trying to support him and ease his pain.

'Those wounds look serious,' she said, and looked at Madeline. 'We'll have to see what we can do.'

'We need to find the keys to get that chain off him,' said Lizzie.

She headed back into the room where Chan had been sleeping – and the first thing she came across was the large book that he'd dropped, lying open on the floor. She knelt down and examined it.

The writing was beautiful, delicate squiggles, curves and slashes of faded black ink in columns down each page. Two of the columns had what appeared to be a kind of stamped mark, a diagram of a mini-maze overlying them. The paper was brittle, like a translucent, pearly shell. The soft leather cover had more refined calligraphy, as well as tiny, exquisite drawings of flowers, trees, and mountains, all surrounding a larger picture of a Chinese-looking lion.

'What is it?' said Madeline, looking over her shoulder.

'I think it's The Book of Life,' said Lizzie.

Chapter 23: Recovery

'Lizzie! Lizzie!'

She woke with a start as her bedroom door swung open and banged against the wall. Next a huge weight landed with a thump on her quilt and before she knew it Mr Tubs was giving her face a thoroughly unwished-for clean with his tongue.

She smiled despite the aches and pains she felt throughout her body, and in her knee in particular.

'Tubs...' she whispered, hugging him round the neck.

Her mum loomed above her.

'Time to get up, Lizzie,' she said. 'You've overslept again.'

'Mum... I think I'm ill,' she groaned.

Her mum eyed her suspiciously, as Tubs tried to worm himself under the quilt with her.

'I'll get the thermometer,' she said, and turned and disappeared out of the room.

'Boy, am I pleased to see you!' said Lizzie, burying her nose in the little dog's fur. 'And *her*...' she added.

She wasn't at all surprised when her mum took her temperature and found it to be high.

Everything had finally caught up with her.

*

She stayed in bed for the next two days, coughing, sweating, sneezing and sleeping. Her mum looked after her meticulously, bringing her tea, soup, biscuits and fruit, and never once suggesting she got up or exerted herself in any way. Mr Tubs stayed constantly on the threadbare mat at her bedside, watching her, cleaning himself, hoping for the occasional stroke, but mostly just sleeping too. The only time she didn't feel completely cocooned and safe was one morning when she heard a car on the drive and realised it was Godwin come to see her mum. But he was gone shortly after, obviously after her mum had explained that Lizzie was ill and she was looking after her. Her mum came upstairs afterwards and mentioned in passing that Godwin had told her that Chen the gardener seemed to have disappeared without a trace, and that he would try and find them another one. Godwin thought it might have something to do with his student visa expiring, perhaps he'd overspent his time in the UK and the authorities had caught up with him.

Slowly, when her head wasn't aching, and as she began to feel less crushingly tired and unwell, she began to absorb what had happened to her. There was much that was really hard to bear, especially the death of Lola and the terrible injuries to Raj. And there was much that seemed too strange to even believe, such as Mr Paterson's distortion of time and his ability to possess ordinary men and boys with the fearsome spirits of the bayou. And then, underlying it all, was another shadow. What exactly had Lamya, Mr Paterson and Chen Yang – and Eva, before she was killed – been up to? Why did they want the Book of Life – and the weird doll, Sally Ally – in the first place? What were they going to do with them? And who was the Englishman that Pandu insisted he had heard both in Sabi's palace and Eva's basement? She had a horrible feeling it was Godwin, whom she hadn't trusted ever since she first saw him on the hunt. But she knew that there was nothing she could do about it. *At least for now.*

And there was one more thing that was troubling her, on an even deeper level.

How do you know something, and yet not know it at the same time?

Right up until he'd left her in the early hours of the morning of that fateful day, Pandu had insisted that she'd appeared to him as some kind of spectre in order to save everyone's skin in Louisiana. But the last she'd remembered before he arrived at Cypress House was falling off the roof in the rain.

Except it wasn't.

There were images, or more accurately, *impressions* of something else in her mind. Like the experience of moving through the tirthas, she could *almost* recall feeling eerie, ultraviolet patches of energy sifting about on a dark and rain-drenched swamp. She had a sense of unworldly and unsafe entities, hanging around the peripheries. And… and she remembered something of a boy, a Chinese boy, and a woman in... in a place that was her garden, but also *wasn't...*

Or perhaps it was all just a dream. But if so, how could Pandu ever have reached her?

She thought about her meeting with Caroline's spirit out on the swamp, on that first night. Was there some unusual connection between the two of them? They were both distantly related.

What could it be?

*

By the weekend she was better, and she managed to take Tubs out for a walk and arrange to meet Ashlyn and Madeline in the bookshop in Hebley that Madeline owned.

It was a mild spring day with a drizzle of rain and a light wind. Stopping beneath the bookshop's swingboard with its picture of a beady-eyed crow, she looked in the window and was surprised to see the two witches talking to a man with a broad-brimmed black hat. He was facing away from her, sitting on a chair and holding a stick.

She decided to go in anyway, the door bell tinkling as she pushed it open. The two witches and the man in the hat turned as she entered.

'Raj!' exclaimed Lizzie, running up and flinging her arms around his neck. She hugged him as hard as she could whilst Mr Tubs licked his fingers around the handle of the stick.

'Oh, steady my dear,' he said, wincing.

She pulled back, and then noticed how ill and drawn he still looked.

'We've been using some of the old herbs – and a little of the old *Wiccan magic* – to do what we can for him,' said Ashlyn. 'But it's no ordinary wound, I'm afraid.'

'And I got injured by the Daginis, remember?' said Raj, finally managing to sound spritely despite his pain. 'I've had more than my fair share of damage from all the devil spawn chucked out by those blasted tirthas!'

Lizzie laughed despite herself. Then she said: 'What do you think they were all up to? The Book, the doll – and Eva, wanting the Lingam so much?'

'I don't know,' said Ashlyn. 'But I'm sure it was something terrible, against the natural order of things. We need to keep our eyes and ears open, just in case Chen returns.'

'Yes,' said Lizzie. 'But at least we know the Lingam – and the doll – are safe now.'

'I'll go back to Kashi,' Raj said. 'I'll keep a watch on Sabi. And of course I need to get back for Albi, who's been staying at my house. Pandu went back to see him, but they'll still need my help – or at least my money to buy some food!

'Plus I've got an employer who's going to need to see a doctor's certificate. An *Indian* doctor's certificate. Otherwise I might end up out of a job!' He winked at Lizzie, then chuckled and winced at the same time.

Madeline spoke to Lizzie. 'We've done everything we can for the Inspector. It's down to normal medicine now, painkillers and such.'

'What will you tell the other policemen?' said Lizzie.

'The truth,' said Raj. 'That I got attacked by a couple of loopy dogs.'

'They'll never believe you,' said Lizzie.

'Who cares? What can they do?' said Raj.

Madeline made them some tea and they sat in the quiet shop talking. Lizzie explained more to them about the people in Louisiana, and what had happened there.

'I told Caroline and Miles that you would go through the tirtha to speak to them,' said Lizzie to Ashlyn. 'I think they could really do with your help right now. There's so much for them to deal with, surfacing from fifty surreal years of hell.

'And then…' she paused. 'And I think... I think Caroline could really do with speaking to you as well about… about leaving her body when she was asleep. About how she met me on the bayou that night – as a *spirit*…'

Lizzie looked up uncertainly into Ashlyn's green eyes.

'Of course,' said the witch. 'I'll tell her all about astral walking, about how it happens – and about what it means if you can do it.' Ashlyn looked at her steadily.

'Thank you,' said Lizzie.

'So what are we going to do about the Book?' said Madeline. 'With its secrets of immortality – we could certainly do with knowing those!'

Lizzie noticed Ashlyn flash the old woman a look of concern.

'Secrets that are entirely useless as no one understands a word they're written in,' said Raj.

'I have an idea,' said Lizzie.

Epilogue: The Barrier of Cloud

It was by far and away one of her favourites.

The *Master of Nets* garden was tucked away behind the gloomy trees and giant hoary gunnera leaves of the Pond garden. It was secluded, but full of gaily painted model buildings, tiny rockeries, exquisite but poorly-looking dwarf trees, and small, bushy plants flowering in all shades of pink and white, soft and lovely like roses without thorns. And there was a small shallow rectangular pool, fed by a runoff channel from the Pond garden, around which everything had been constructed.

With their delicate lattice windows and little pointed roofs with flying eaves, the buildings were clearly meant to be Chinese. Or possibly Japanese, she conceded. *But she hoped they were Chinese.*

They – *she and Ashlyn* – had so far discovered very little about this garden from the journals. In fact, the only entries mentioning it were to do with the plants her great-uncle Eric had added to it and how he'd managed some of the diseases that had affected them. There had been nothing about a tirtha.

Which didn't mean there wasn't one, of course. Simply that either he hadn't found it, or that they hadn't found it within the thousands of pages of dreadful handwriting which constituted the record of his life at Rowan Cottage and through the tirthas.

So now she would see if she could find one. She'd already spent several hours on the last few weekends making futile attempts, Mr Tubs snuffling around as she pushed her index finger into minute doorways and windows, lifted up roofs, shifted stones about, and stepped adroitly on and in between the incy wincy rockeries. As normal, to no avail.

But then last night she had had a dream. A dream whose images had entirely vanished when she woke in the morning, but which had left her with three clear words in her mind. *Barrier of Cloud.*

She'd hurried downstairs and turned on the tablet she'd finally persuaded her mum to buy for them to share. Within moments she was on the web, searching for the term.

And now she was standing here, clearing away shrubbery that had grown up in front of a small wall of yellowish rocks at one edge of the pool. A wall of rocks that she now knew was meant to resemble a gentle mist rising above the water.

The Barrier of Cloud.

Before stepping over the miniature wall, she picked up the large book that she'd set down on top of one of the little buildings.

Mr Tubs yapped once, twice as she said goodbye.

*

As usual, things swim. Dragons, long red scales sweeping through white rolling waves, gold and yellow with huge, curious eyes, and other beasts, beasts with fangs and sharp black hair surrounding their glaring faces, a thousand, million, trillion simple repeated words, poems, bamboo and mountains, proud horses frothing at the mouth, countless men with swords marching, blood, more blood, and more gold, and beneath it all a long, low, steady sound, om...

*

She was on her knees, her face in her hands, like one who had just suffered.

But she was OK, she felt fine.

She was getting better at this, something to do with acceptance, not fighting the fear and strangeness of the transportation.

She took her hands away from her face and looked up.

She was in a place of beauty. Before her was water, brown and green and silver with reflections of the trees, rocks and sky that rose above it. Two red wooden bridges arched gracefully across the pool as it wended away from her between jutting rocks. One of the bridges ran into an open pagoda, with delicately pointed eaves. A gentle, ethereal mist hung over everything, softening the reflections and muting the reds, yellows and greens of the leaves on the trees. Off to her right, she noticed through the trees and bushes that the landscape fell away sharply, that the garden was in fact on a mountainside – although how high up she was, was impossible to tell because of the mist.

She breathed in the clear, chill air, and its earthy scents of water and rock. She picked up the book that had come through with her, and began to walk along a gravel path that ran towards the first bridge, in between fine trees and the shiny grey rocks at the pool's edge.

She reached the first bridge, crossed over it, and made her way along a small path between silvery grasses and russet coloured bushes, past a ledge that fell precipitously away between two larger trees into the mist below – *how long was that drop?* – and then around and back on to the second bridge which led up to the pagoda.

There was someone in the pagoda, sitting on a seat and looking away from her, into the fog that shrouded the mountain. She reached the end of the bridge and climbed the two steps up into the small building, which smelt of dusty wood.

The person – completely bald, dressed in a saffron robe – still hadn't looked around.

'Hello,' she said, holding the book against her front.

It was an old man, who stood up and turned round when he heard her.

'Hello,' he said, in accented English.

He was a Chinese man, very, very old, with nut-brown skin and delighted eyes. He frowned, as if struggling with recognition, then smiled and exclaimed: 'It's you!'

He walked over to her quickly and grasped her arms, grinning and showing all his teeth.

'After all these years...' he said. 'Whoever would have thought it? I'm so happy to see you again!'

'And me you,' she said.

'You had more of a... *glow* about you last time,' he said.

'You've grown – more than I'd imagined!'

'Yes, I had a growth spurt in my teens,' he said, laughing. 'But the *L'il* bit stuck with me all my life. You know people...'

Lizzie nodded, smiling. She realised she had hardly ever felt so happy.

Then she held the book up to him.

'I was wondering if you could translate this for me?' she said.

'I can have a go,' he said.

Thank you for reading my book. If you enjoyed it, please help spread the word by writing a review.

Lizzie's adventures continue in…

The Dreamer Falls

A mysterious garden full of portals in the English countryside.

An ancient book, warning of supernatural beings preying on humankind.

A missing boy – and a girl who has seen too much.

Living with the secret of the tirthas is getting too much for Lizzie Jones. Even when her friend Xing warns her of the plans of the evil beings using the portals, she decides she's had enough. After all, they've defeated all the demons, haven't they?

Then Lizzie finds a discarded phone by an African mask in one of the gardens. The phone of local village boy Thomas Bennett, who recently disappeared.

Once again, Lizzie must act – but what can she do?

All five books in The Secret of the Tirthas are now available on Amazon:

Book 1: The City of Light
Book 3: The Dreamer Falls
Book 4: The Lady in the Moon Moth Mask
Book 5: The Unknown Realms

Also available

The Boy in the Burgundy Hood – *a ghost story*

Poetry:

Up in the Air

Author's Note – *Origins of The Secret of the Tirthas*

It's a very long time since I went to Louisiana as a 13-year-old with my dad so I have to be honest, most of this book is written on the basis of research, with a healthy dose of imagination thrown in, as opposed to recall. I do however remember the humidity, the exotic liveliness and spiritedness of New Orleans mixing French, Spanish, African and American in with a whole lot more.

When I was a small boy I developed an early taste for gothic and used to persuade my parents to let me (like Lizzie) sit up and watch horror films, during which (like Lizzie) I would fall asleep nine times out of ten. I also started writing my own adventure stories putting school friends in lead roles, which got them passed around class and gave me a taste for writing for others' as opposed to just my own pleasure. But for some reason I stopped writing in my late teens and didn't start again until after university, when my focus became poetry. I published poems in a variety of magazines, including *Poetry Ireland, New Welsh Review, Magma* and *The Rialto*. Then my wife's parents bought a cottage in Herefordshire with a marvellous *garden of rooms*, themed around different cultures and periods. It was a unique and inspirational place and soon I was putting ideas together with my previous travels, including to India and Louisiana, and with my love of gothic, and then I had the concept for *The Secret of the Tirthas*.

I want to thank some of the many people who helped me write the first two books. My mother- and father-in-law, Janet and David Martin, who bought, tended and developed the garden (plus cottage) that inspired the setting, and who have read and reviewed the books more than enough times. My friend Brian Ruckley, with whom I spent many evenings discussing the pleasures of writing and who proved it could all be more than just a pipe dream. The Child family, who helped me out particularly with a great image when I was stuck. My wonderful mum, who has been a constant bedrock and who has always nurtured and encouraged my desire to write. And finally my wife Anna, who has been editor, proof-reader, promoter, chief enthuser, regular guardian of exuberant small children, and much, much more besides.

If you want to be the first to hear about new books, you can subscribe to my mailing list at: stevegriffin40@outlook.com

To find out more about me and see photos of the garden and other settings that inspired *The Secret of the Tirthas*, check out steve-griffin.com. You can also find me on Facebook and Instagram under my profile @stevegriffin.author.

Printed in Great Britain
by Amazon

56025458R00144